To All Our Children

JIM   •   JANE   •   JOHN

JOSIE *and* JOHN

&

EMILY

designed & illustrated by BETTY BEEBY

Whistle up the Bay

by

NANCY STONE

WM. B. EERDMANS PUBLISHING COMPANY
GRAND RAPIDS, MICHIGAN

Set up and printed, April 1966
Reprinted, February 1979

contents

A Message to the Reader

Betty Beeby, who did the wonderful illustrations for this book, discovered the story of Theo, Tommy, and Herman. For many years she had been searching for a tale of the Grand Traverse region that could be made into a book. She read old diaries, almanacs, letters, newspapers, and books. She talked to the children of the settlers, now grown old themselves, and finally to Mrs. Grace Hooper. Mrs. Hooper is the daughter of one of the boys whose story is told in this book. She, too, had collected tales of the early days and one of the stories she recorded was that of her own father and his two brothers. When Mrs. Beeby heard the story of these three sturdy immigrants, she felt she had discovered the chronicle for which she had been searching.

6

She came to me in the summer of 1964 and asked me if I would be interested in writing the story of the Escher boys. I, too, became absorbed in the region and its history and decided that of all the people who might enjoy such a narrative the boys and girls of the same age as our three heroes would be most appreciative of the meaning of their hardships.

Most of the book is true, in one way or another. The main events of the story actually happened pretty much as I have written them. The background and incidental material is as representative as possible, and the smaller incidents either did happen or could have happened.

All the other characters in the book are fictional. They do not even resemble anyone I know. Also, I have changed the boys' last name, but, frankly, we came to love them so by their real first names that changing those was virtually impossible.

In addition to Mrs. Hooper's notes and the background material loaned me by Mrs. Beeby, the Kalamazoo Public Library proved to have a fine collection of material about Michigan and I am grateful to all of these people for giving me such free access to their resources.

If you should ever go to Antrim County, you will find an Antrim City there, but it is not the one in this book. The Antrim of the long pier has been gone for many years, buried under the sands of the beach. The foundations of the pier are still there, under the cold, blue waters of the bay. They can still be seen, in fact.

We hope you will go there some day, and see for yourself the country that shaped these very young immigrants and that was, in turn, shaped by them.

NANCY STONE

Here in the forest
three boys were orphaned
and met the challenge
of the wilderness
alone

1

A Bucket of Flour

"Ho, there, boys!"

Theo shaded his eyes and looked out over the water. A fisherman stood in a flat-bottomed boat, a little way out from the beach. The sun behind him was low in the sky across Grand Traverse Bay. Theo found it hard to see the man's face clearly.

Tommy called loudly,

"Hi! What do you want?" Then he ran toward the water's edge, the cold, choppy water sucking under his bare feet. Theo waved, but stayed where he was. Herman stood silently behind him.

"I've got something you might like to have," the man called. Just then, a white-capped wave caught the prow of his boat, and, swaying dangerously, the fisherman sat down quickly and started to row toward the beach.

The boys, all three of them at the water now, watched the small craft coming in.

"What is it, d'ya s'pose?" asked Tommy.

"How should I know," said Theo.

Tommy danced up and down and pulled his hands as far as they would go into the sleeves of his rough, home-spun jacket.

"Gettin' cold," he said, "must be close to suppertime. How much have we got now?" He looked up the little stream, not far from where they stood. Half an hour earlier they had left their wild plum picking and come down to the beach at the place where the stream flowed into the bay.

"About a peck, I guess," said Theo. He looked anxiously as the boat came close. When, finally, the prow swished onto the sand, he ran forward and grabbed the rope tied to the boat's nose.

"Hold tight there, sonny," said the fisherman.

"Yessir," said Theo.

"Here, take this one, boy," the man said to Tommy, who had run up to the side of the boat. He dropped a big white flour sack into Tommy's arms. The boy staggered a little.

"It's wet," he exclaimed.

"Yup. Go put that one up on the beach and come back, I'll give you another. Let's keep moving along now." He dropped another sack on the wet sand, near Theo's feet. Herman tried to lift it, but finally used his small hands to pull it slowly back to where Tommy had dropped the first sack. Theo continued to hold the boat's rope.

"You can let go now, lad, and help your brothers," said the fisherman. He threw another sack on the wet sand, and Theo dropped the line to pick up the damp burden.

Back and forth the boys worked, silently, as the fisherman, now and then calling encouragement, threw sack after sack out of his boat. When a dozen sacks lay safely on the dry sand, the man climbed out of his boat.

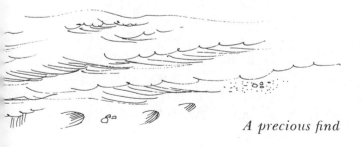

A precious find

"You the Escher boys, ain't ya?"

"Yessir," answered Tommy quickly.

"Pa still sick?" asked the man.

"Yes, he is," said Theo.

"I'm Joshua Snow," the fisherman said. "Live down this side o' Torch Lake, but I came over t' the bay to get whitefish."

"I'm Tommy, and that's Theodore and that's Herman," said Tommy, grinning at Mr. Snow.

"How old are ya?" asked Mr. Snow.

"I'm twelve," said Tommy. "Theo is fourteen and Herman is only six."

"But what's in the sacks, Mr. Snow?" asked Theo impatiently.

"Wal, boys, there's flour in them sacks."

"But it's wet," stated Herman.

"Oh, ho," said Mr. Snow, "We'll see about that." He pulled a knife from his pocket. Then, starting to rip the sacking of one of the wet bundles, he paused.

"Got a clean, dry bucket, or something like that?" he asked.

The boys looked at each other a moment and then Herman's face brightened. He ran without a word to where the buckets of wild plums were sitting, beside the stream, near the underbrush. He dumped the plums on the sand without hesitating and ran back with the empty bucket. When he got back, he looked around hesitatingly for a moment and then Mr. Snow spoke.

"Here, lad, give it to me." He took the pail and dipping up some dry sand, swished it around inside the damp bucket. Then he took from his neck an enormous red handkerchief and wiped out all the sand. The pail was dry. He finished ripping a hole in the sack of flour. Wet flour flowed onto the sand, crumbled and plopped onto the sand, but inside was a core, probably two or three cups, of dry, undamaged flour. The boys looked jubilantly at each other.

"Look!" shouted Tommy, "flour!"

"For us, Mr. Snow?" asked Theo.

Herman started carefully scooping the dry flour into the pail.

"Yep. For you, boys. I heard your pa was ailing and I thought maybe you could use it."

"But where did it come from?" asked Theo.

"Oh, from the *Lakeside*, I reckon. She went aground on Fox Island last week, carryin' a load of flour and they likely dumped some over to lighten her enough to get off."

"Thank you, Mr. Snow," said Herman, remembering his manners.

"That's all right, boy. Give my regards to your pa."

Mr. Snow stood up, huge in his grimy mackinaw and knitted cap. He folded his knife, and put it back in his pocket. He grinned at the boys and stumped across the sand to his boat. His knee-high boots flapped around his legs, slapped against each other at every step. He pushed the small craft into the water and jumped in quickly. Taking the oars, he headed the boat toward Antrim City. The boys could see, around the curve of the beach, the long dark finger of the Antrim Pier, a couple of miles away.

Tommy waved enthusiastically and called, "Thanks, Mr. Snow!"

Mr. Snow waved once to the brothers standing beside the pile of wet sacks.

"We'd better get the dry flour out and home," said Theo.

"How'll we cut the sacks?" asked Tommy.

15

Herman looked around and found a broken stick with which he tore a jagged hole in the side of one sack. Carefully he pushed and scooped away the wet and slimy flour around the center of usable flour.

Theo and Tommy dropped to the sand beside him and copied his operation. Before they had finished, the sun was very low and red across the bay. Around the place where they worked, gulls were talking with curiosity about them and pecking with leisurely dignity at the outer bits of wet flour.

When the boys finished, the pail was almost full. They looked at each other with satisfaction. They started up the beach, Theo and Herman carrying the bucket between them, brushing with their hands at the sandy flour that clung to their trousers.

Tommy ran ahead to the pile of plums they had left beside the stream.

"How'll we carry these?" he shouted. "I know," he answered himself. "Take off your jacket, Theo."

Theo hesitated a minute and then, looking at Herman, he dropped his side of the pail handle. Herman lowered the bucket to the ground with a thump.

Theo took off his jacket and handed it to Tommy.

"Why mine, I'd like to know?"

"Because Herman's is too small and mine has a hole in the back. A big hole." Tommy laughed gaily and flung the jacket on the ground. He scrabbled the plums onto the jacket and taking hold of the bottom corners and the collar, he slung it over his shoulder.

"*Now!* It's over the mountain track with our knapsacks, lads!" he called.

Herman laughed and jumped up and down.

"Tommy, stop," said Theo, "we must get home to Father. It'll be suppertime and he'll need more hot coals for the warming pan."

"I *am* going home, Theo. You're so touchy," Tommy said and plodded up the banks of the stream. Theo and Herman lifted the pail between them again and followed Tommy into the thicket. Around them a few tall hemlocks and maples rose, but there were not many full-grown trees between the boys and the top of the bluff which sloped down to meet the beach. Here, near the course of the stream, the slope was gentle. Farther along the beach, the bluff was steep. A few pine seedlings struggled up, only a few feet tall, through the underbrush of blackberries and wild cherry and here and there a thicket of sumac. Close to the stream red osier hung its neat green leaves and shimmering, rosy bark.

"Why do they cut down the tall trees?" asked Herman.

"For lumber," said Theo absently, watching Tommy trudge exaggeratedly ahead of them.

"But where do they take it?"

"Chicago, I guess. How should I know?"

Herman fell silent.

When they reached the top of the bluff, they rested a moment. Theo and Herman gently set the pail on the softness of what had once been forest floor. Around them, scattered thickly through the undergrowth, were the trunks of fallen trees. Some of them were without their limbs, but many had dead branches thrusting into the air at wild angles.

Running along the beach at the top of the bluff was a wide swath cut in the underbrush and through the

17

trees. It was traced with ruts and beaten flat by ox carts and stone boats and sledges and by logs, pulled endlessly, two by two, by oxen or by huge, stamping horses down to the edge of a smaller lake to be started on the long and winding journey to the sawmills and lumber ships at Elk Rapids. This was the Flat Road. The settlers themselves had cleared the land for it, and some day, some day, it would be paved for buggies and carriages to use.

Across the cleared track and a little north, a thin column of smoke rose into the flawless sky. The roof of the house from which it came was very low, hidden by three or four tall pines.

"The fire's still goin', anyway," remarked Tommy.

"Yes, but suppose it went out and Father had to get up and build it again," said Theo.

"Now, why think that, Theo? It was a good fire, I built it myself," said Tommy.

Herman giggled and looked from one brother to the other.

"Well, we'll soon see," said Theo and motioned for Herman to pick up his side of the pail handle. They trudged up the road and Tommy followed with his coat full of plums.

2
Papa Escher

The three boys reached a farmyard clearing in the second-growth forest. A small, shingled cabin, new and raw, stood there. When they reached the door, Tommy lowered the packet to the ground and started at a trot toward a rail-fenced clearing up a slope behind the barn.

"Hey!" shouted Herman, "you forgot the milk pail!"

Tommy turned and ran back as Herman stepped inside the door and came out a moment later with a blue granite pail. He handed it to Tommy, who started off again.

Theo looked thoughtfully after his brother.

"I hope we have enough food for the cow this winter," he said.

"Papa's waiting, Theo. Let's go in," said Herman. He tugged at the handle of the pail they still held between them.

The room they entered was about twelve feet wide and twenty feet long. Here they cooked and ate. At one end was a door to the only other room on the ground floor, a small dark bedroom for their father. The three boys slept in the wide loft, reached by a roughly built ladder. There were two small windows in the east wall opposite the door. Now they were almost dark. The sun still streamed in the door, ruddy and warm, as the boys came in.

"Papa," called Theo, "we are home!"

"Theo," came a voice from the bedroom. "Come here, son. Where have you been?"

Theo and Herman hurried into the bedroom with their precious pail of flour.

"Look, Papa, look," said Herman, and jumped up and down beside the simple, low bed in which their father lay. He was a man slightly more than fifty. Now he was thin, but his shoulders were broad and the bones in his hands strong.

"Father," began Theo.

"Papa, Papa!" shouted Herman.

"Boys! Quiet! One at a time, please." He spoke with dignity, but his voice was weak. The boys were quiet immediately and then Theo began to tell the tale of their burden. When they had finished, their father smiled.

"My sons," he said, "I believe it will be all right for us to accept the help of Mr. Snow. I do not usually like to take such help, as you know, but he was only hastening something we might have had anyway. After all, the bags would have floated in by themselves and been on the beach for your gathering."

"Yes, Papa," said the boys together. Theo understood what his father was saying. He had heard it many times, said in many ways, before this. Herman did not understand completely, but he furrowed his brow, trying to do so.

"Where is Thomas?" asked their father.

"Milking the cow, Father," said Theo.

"Of course, of course."

"How is your back, Papa?" asked Herman.

"Ah, Herman," he said, "it is better today, thank you."

He spoke with a heavy German accent, although he seemed to know English well. Jacob Escher was a Swiss immigrant who had come to America eleven years before, and to this part of Michigan four years ago, a year after the end of the Civil War. This was the frontier he had come to find. Here man's hand was less visible. Lumbering had slashed its mark upon the landscape, but not as heavily as on the Eastern shores of the state. The grand beauties of the forest still rose, here and there, on the eighty-acre piece of land that was their homestead. Bit by bit they cleared their farm and planted crops, each year a little more. Sometimes this small part of the frontier seemed unfriendly and sinister, in spite of its beauties. In the spring, while finishing the house in which he now lay ill, Jacob had injured his back; the injury had become inflamed and he had lingered in pain and desperation all through the long summer, while his boys had cleared more land, planted some crops, and taken care of all the other things there were to do on a wilderness farm.

Now he was improving. His back had almost stopped hurting and the doctor from Traverse City who had come through two weeks before had said he would be on his feet and good as new before the snow came.

Now he enjoyed having his sons ask him how he felt,

so he had answered Herman jovially and patted the small boy tenderly on his rough black hair.

"I'm so glad, Papa," said Herman.

"Yes, Papa, it is good that you are improving," said Theo.

"Now, boys, it is late, time we were eating dinner. Tonight we will make bread and tomorrow we will dine royally." He settled the quilt that covered him neatly under his arms and the boys went into the main room of the cabin.

"Try to find something to cover this, or the mice will be at it, Herman," said Theo regally, as he lifted the bucket of flour to the rough pine table that stood before the fireplace at one end of the room. Herman glared at him a moment and then went to a cupboard in the corner and took from it another granite pan, looked at the pail, inverted the pan over the pail and stood back with satisfaction when the pan fit perfectly over the precious contents of the pail.

Meanwhile, Theo had taken a pan of corn meal, which he had ground himself that summer, from the cupboard. As he salted the meal, he said, "Herman, go get me some milk."

"Oh, Theo, not your johnnycakes again," he wailed.

"What do you want, your highness, some of your delicious bread, I suppose." Herman looked hurt, and left without another word. Theo had touched a sore spot. Herman never remembered to put salt in the bread, and his father had sadly whipped him for it, time after time.

Herman went to the well at one corner of the house and, cranking up the bucket, took from it a covered pail of milk. Their father did not like to have them use warm milk, fresh from their cow, so he did not even consider waiting for Tommy when he saw him coming across the farmyard with a pail of foaming milk.

"Johnnycakes, I s'pose!" called Tommy.

Herman just nodded his head.

"Well, tomorrow you can make us some bread," said Tommy, and laughed.

That night for supper the boys and their father ate a familiar meal: eggs, wild plums, potatoes, fried with the eggs in bacon drippings, and, covered with their own maple syrup, corn-meal patties called johnnycakes. A neighbor who had come from New England had taught Theo how to make johnnycakes. With this simple meal they drank coffee, hot and fragrant with chicory.

After supper they washed the tin plates and cups and went in to sit beside their father until bedtime, a single candle on the floor of the dim room, the kitchen fire throwing occasional bright shadows around the corner and into the bedroom door.

Usually, these were not happy times for the boys, nor for Jacob Escher. There were too many regrets and sad times in the past and too few joys apparent for the future. But tonight there was a lightness in the air as Herman helped Theo roll a big log to the fireplace and heave it into place. Then Herman brushed the hearth neatly, and followed his brothers into his father's room.

Father settled himself comfortably on his bed. "Tomorrow you can dig potatoes, boys."

"Yes, Papa," said Tommy.

". . . and then take some into town to Samuel."

"Yes, Papa!" shouted Herman at this treat.

Their father chuckled.

The three boys sat with faces glowing in the candlelight and the flickers from the fire in the other room.

Through the tiny windows at the end of the bedroom

23

there was nothing to see but the blackness of the night. The wind had risen from across the bay and they could hear, very faintly and very far away, the slap of waves on the shore. The autumn storms were brewing.

Father sighed.

"Are you in pain, Father?" asked Theo.

"Only in my spirit, son," said Jacob.

"Why, Father? What do you mean? We thought you were getting well," said Tommy.

"I am, son, in my body, but when I think of the long winter nights ahead, I remember with such pain the beautiful books we lost and how much they would relieve the cold, dark tedium of these northern nights."

Herman did not understand all of this, but he felt the sorrow in his father's voice, and put his hand tenderly on his father's own. His father smiled at him.

"Do not fret, my lad. You will go to school and learn to read yourself. Then, some day we will have more books and you will read them to me, then."

"Yes, Papa," said Herman.

"Father," said Tommy, "tell us how we came here."

"But, Thomas, I have told you that story time and again.".

Even so, he told them the long story again. How he, Jacob Escher, then forty, had left his respected job as

24

manager of a workman's cooperative in Zurich, among the pleasant crags of Switzerland, and come, with wife and three children — Bertha, Theodore and Thomas — to the malarial swamps of Missouri. There the mother had died, after Herman was born, and there Bertha suffered from malaria, so that a few years later, after they had decided to come to Michigan, Bertha, too, had died. She was buried on the little hill behind the barn. Now, Theo, Tommy, and Herman had been in charge of the farm since spring. Only two years before, their house had burned to the ground, destroying all the precious books — their father had read both French and German — and the mementoes and keepsakes that had come on the dangerous journey across the Altantic some ten years before.

"I like the ocean voyage best," said Tommy.

"Well, you didn't like it then, I can tell you," said Theo.

"Neither did you, I'll bet," said Tommy.

"Boys, boys," said their father, "none of us enjoyed the voyage in that way. Our bodies were uncomfortable and sick, but our souls were glad to be going to a free, adventurous land."

"Yes, Papa," said Theo and Tommy together.

"Papa," asked Herman, "will you tell us again the games you played when you were a little boy?"

Jacob patted Herman on the head and Tommy looked angrily at his little brother.

"He's old enough to forget about children's play," said Tommy.

Their father laughed.

"Time enough to be a man when he has been a boy," he said.

"Yes, Papa," grumbled Tommy, and Theo kicked

him lightly on the leg, under cover of the dim candle-light. Tommy kicked him back.

"Well, Herman," began his father, "one of the things we liked to do best was pretend mountain climbing."

"Yes, Papa," Herman said, his eyes shining.

"I lived on a farm for a while when I was a boy, and in the back of the house was a huge pile of manure, saved through the winter to spread on the fields in the spring. By this time of the year, it had already grown to quite a height. We would strap small bundles, although they seemed large to us, on our backs, grasp our homemade alpenstocks and mattocks and climb laboriously to the top of that pile of manure. It was lovely to be first on the rope and the first to raise the cry of 'Success!' when we reached the top. To be a mountain guide was, for us, the kind of ambition you American boys . . ." — he stopped here and smiled with pride at his sons — ". . . have when you want to be Indian scouts."

"What did you have in the packs?" asked Tommy.

"Oh, not much. Usually, some stones and some hay. It was more difficult to climb with packs and made us prouder when we reached the top."

He sighed heavily.

"Papa, it's time we let you sleep," said Theo. "Come along boys. We have a very busy day tomorrow."

"Good night, Papa," Tommy said and kissed his father warmly.

"Good night, Papa," said Herman with a hug.

"Good night, Father," said Theo. He shuffled his feet for a moment, then put out his hand. His father, smiling, shook the hand once, then patted it gently.

"Good night, son. Good night, boys. Please put out the candle as you leave."

26

"Small bundles on our backs"

As Tommy started toward it, Herman quickly blew out the flame.

The next morning, after a simple breakfast, the boys went out to the potato field.

Tommy leaned for a moment on the handle of his shovel at the edge of the field.

"Why don't we divide Herman up? I'll start here, with him helping me, and then, in a while, he can come to help you at the other end."

"All right," said Theo. Herman glared at both of them for a moment.

"All right," he said, and kicked the basket on the ground beside him.

"Be careful, son," said Tommy gently.

"Don't call me that. I'm not your son."

"Oh, go along and help," said Tommy, pushing him roughly after Theo, who was carefully picking his way down to the opposite end of the field.

The field, once part of the ancient forest, was poorly cleared. Many stumps dotted its uneven surface, only a few of them uprooted, ready to be moved. There was not space enough for more than two or three potato plants to form a real row. Instead, the bushy green plants seemed dotted at random over the small field, many of them nestling comfortably at the base of massive stumps.

The boys worked steadily in the morning sun. Their jackets lay here and there on stumps. Gradually, their baskets filled. The potatoes were small and rather lumpy, but they were ripe and sound. In two hours they had their three baskets filled, sorted, and repacked into six smaller bags.

"Do we have time to go into town today?" called Tommy.

"Yes," said Theo, "I think we'd better."

"Yes, I think so, too," said Tommy with a nod of his head.

Leaving three of the bags in the barn, the two older boys each lifted a heavy sack to his shoulders. Herman had run to the barn a few minutes before and now came back with a small, rattly wooden wagon, whose wheels had been fastened to their axles with wire, now quite rusty. Tommy helped him lift the sack to his wagon. The boys set off down the rough trail toward Antrim, the nearest town.

Here and there a hillside difficult to log would still be dark with tall, old trees. The deep dark green of late summer still held sway in the scattered forests and the dense scrub growth that covered the logged-off barrens. Beside the trail, and now and then in it, the boys stepped among the varied yellows of St. John's wort and pushed aside tall, thriving ironweed, grand in its purple thistle-like flowers. Bluejays and crows called in the woods.

Occasionally the boys would come to a pile of huge trees, fallen and tangled together, near the trail. Sometimes a blue racer would be sunning himself on a warm gray log.

"Let's rest a minute," said Theo, after they had gone almost a mile. Tommy silently lowered his sack to the ground. Herman pulled his wagon beside a huge stone and sat down. Theo and Tommy stretched out on the ground beside the trail. For several minutes none of them said anything.

"These have been good days," said Theo at last.

"Ummm," said Tommy sleepily.

"Why?" asked Herman.

"Well, we've gotten lots of things to help us when winter comes, lots of things to eat, that is."

"Yes, but there's still all the wood to chop." Tommy remembered sadly that a big job lay ahead of him.

"Yes," said Herman, "and if you don't work faster on it, we'll be cold this winter." He shivered.

"I will, I will, but there's always so much to do." Tommy turned over in the sun and sat up.

"Let's go," said Theo.

They heaved their sacks to their shoulders and went on.

Now they passed a house, crude and glowering among the scrub. There were racks behind the house, draped with fishing nets. Leander Boyle took his share of the wilderness's bounty from the waters of the lakes. He lived alone, with three cats. They lay in a row on the eaves now, basking in the sun.

After another mile, the boys turned down a branch of the trail in the direction of the bay. The trail led downward, through sand dunes covered only in spots with beach grass and low evergreens. The trail they were on now was paved with logs, run side by side across the trail.

29

It was called a corduroy road and was cheap paving in this land of the pine. They could see, over the dunes, the smoke from several chimneys. The trail took its last dip downward, around the side of a menacing dune and there before them lay the town of Antrim.

3
A Sale and a Fight

"There aren't any ships at all today," said Herman with disappointment.

Tommy and Theo lowered their sacks to the ground and the three boys stood a moment, scanning the bay and the long pier that reached far out into the sparkling waters.

"They're down aways today, loading across from Mc-Davitt's," said Tommy.

The boys picked up their burdens and started down the road again. On the left was the small, square Antrim schoolhouse. The door was open and as the boys passed, very slowly, they could see several women inside, brooms and rags in their hands, scrubbing floors and desks and blackboards. In the schoolyard several children were playing, swinging from a rope that hung from a tall white pine, or absorbed in a noisy game of hide-and-seek in the woodshed behind the schoolhouse. Herman sighed.

"Herman should go to school," said Theo firmly.

Tommy snorted.

"We need him, you know it, and how would he get here, and we don't have the money, and. . . ."

"He should go," Theo repeated.

"You think I could, Theo?" asked Herman.

"It's hard work, you know," said Theo turning on him fiercely. "It isn't all play and fun and getting out of chores."

"I know," said Herman, and shifted the handle of his cart to the other hand.

They walked on in silence, passing two or three gray shingled houses, low and bare-looking.

"But . . . you should learn to read," said Theo.

"Everyone should," said Tommy in a very low voice.

Behind them they heard the clatter of horses' hooves and they stepped quickly aside, without looking back. A rumbling farm wagon, drawn by a single horse, passed them. In the back were several boys.

Herman reached down for a stone

"Looka th' dirty 'tater diggers!" one screamed as the wagon bounced past.

"Yeah!!" screamed the others.

Herman reached down for a stone and before Theo could stop him, he had thrown it at the wagon, hitting the tail gate.

The boys in the wagon shouted louder and one threw a very dry old corncob back at Herman, his aim falling short by several feet. By this time the wagon was well down the road, passing the small Baptist church that stood close to the road at the upper end of the main street's row of stores and businesses.

"Herman, you'd better watch out, you know. Papa doesn't want us to fight and there's only two of us, so we couldn't help you very much," said Tommy uneasily.

"Who cares," said Herman. "I could lick 'em."

Theo looked sternly at both the boys.

"We're here on business," he said, "let's act like it."

Now they went by the blacksmith's and the foundry building and came to the wooden sidewalk under the balcony of the small hotel. They walked slowly by the butcher shop, where they could see Mr. McDavitt inside, deftly trimming the fat from a haunch of beef. Herman's mouth watered visibly.

"Maybe we could have a chicken for Sunday dinner," said Tommy in a wistful voice.

Theo had reached the door of the Antrim General Store by now. He stopped and waved to the boys to follow him inside.

"What'll I do with this wagon, Theo?" whispered Herman.

Theo thought for a moment, glancing from the cart to the dark inside of the store.

"Well, better bring it along inside, I guess," he said

33

and held the door open for Herman, who tugged the heavy cart over the threshold and onto the waxed, unpainted floor within.

Two men standing at a high counter near the front window looked at them as they entered. Both of the men were wearing hats and high, rough leather boots. Theo and Herman knew them as logging bosses from Elk Rapids.

The boys stood awkwardly near the door for a moment. Tommy put his sack on the floor and then picked it up again, right away. Two men in white aprons were talking together quietly in the back of the store and paid no attention to the three boys.

"Hello, boys," said a pleasant voice behind them. They turned to see Rev. Brownlow enter. He was a tall, strong-looking man with his rich voice soft as he spoke.

"Hello, sir," they said together.

"Here to sell potatoes?"

"Yes, sir," answered Theo. He glanced anxiously at the two men in the back of the store.

"Samuelll!" called Rev. Brownlow in a full, booming tone.

One of the white-aproned men turned quickly and came toward the front of the store at a trot.

"Yes, Reverend," he said with a broad smile, "can I help you this morning?"

"Later, perhaps, but these boys were ahead of me and I think you might find it good business to deal with them." His voice was jolly and he gave Herman's head a brisk rub or two.

"Yes, of course," said the man called Samuel. The smile faded from his face. He lifted Theo's sack to the counter and opened it. The two logging bosses joined the group and as the store clerk put a few potatoes on

The Antrim General Store

the counter, they each picked one up and examined it carefully.

"Well, they're pretty small," said Samuel.

Theo grew red and said nothing. The four men looked at him expectantly. Finally, Herman spoke.

"They're sound, though, and ripe," he said. All four men smiled.

"That's right, son. Learn to sell what you've got to sell."

"Even religion, eh, Reverend," said one of the loggers.

"That's right, that's right," said Rev. Brownlow and laughed.

His congregation had struggled forlornly before he came. He had been in Antrim only five years, but already his church was larger and more vigorous.

"Well, I'll give you seven cents a peck," said Samuel.

Theo and Tommy looked at each other and finally Theo nodded agreement. The clerk measured out the potatoes and handed Herman the empty sacks to take back in the wagon.

"That'll be forty-two cents. 'Spect you'd like that in goods, am I right?"

"Yessir," said Theo, assuming a businesslike air. The loggers and Rev. Brownlow moved away and talked together at the front window.

"Well, what'll it be?"

"A bag of sugar, some salt, tea, and a bottle of linament for Papa's back."

Samuel hurried around the store, collecting the things Theo had asked for and finally, after gathering them on the counter, wrapped the salt, the tea, and the linament in one small bundle and pushed the sugar and the bundle across to them.

"You still have five cents coming. Shall I put on the books?"

Herman looked at a jar of sourballs and Tommy answered quickly, "Yes, please. You'd better." Samuel laughed and, pulling a small notebook from his hip pocket, wrote something on one of the pages.

Herman, with a sigh, loaded their packages onto the wagon and started out of the store. As Theo and Tommy followed, Rev. Brownlow called after them.

"Boys," he said, "just a minute." He stepped out the door with the three. "How's your father?" he asked.

"Better, thank you, sir. He thinks he'll be up for Christmas."

"That's a long pull for you boys," said Rev. Brownlow soberly.

"We'll be all right, sir," said Theo.

"Well, if you need help, please remember that I am here to help anyone in need."

"Yes, sir," said Tommy without expression.

"I won't urge you to come to Sunday school, because I know your father's beliefs are different from mine, but I am his friend, and tell him I will come to see him one day soon."

"Thank you, sir, we will," said Herman.

"Good-bye, boys."

"Good-bye, sir."

Theo, Tommy, and Herman, pulling his wagon after him, wandered down the main street of Antrim. Down by the water were huge piles of stone and massive logs. These were being used to build the second Antrim City pier. Reaching out into the bay, its builders hoped that it, also, would beckon ships to the city. Schooners, barks, brigantines, and steamers crossed the head of Traverse Bay on their way to or from Chicago. Many went down the west arm to Traverse City to load fruit, perhaps, and probably lumber, or to unload the countless things a frontier town needs from civilization, which was so many miles away over the inland seas. Ships also came down the east arm of Traverse Bay to Elk Rapids to load lumber. Many of them stopped at Antrim, since the pier had been built some five years before. This year there had been almost as many steamers as sailing ships on the bay.

Once they had seen a new kind of steamer, very long, low, and narrow. It had not come into Antrim, but had passed south, probably on its way to a blast furnace. Leander had told them he thought the captain had

missed the turning into the west arm. Leander thought
lake captains were a wild and irresponsible bunch.

The boys gazed out over Antrim's harbor and the bay.
The sawmill not far from the pier sent its noise and
smoke over the little town. The day was hazy and not
even the top of a mast or a bent column of smoke that
meant a ship could be seen on the lake. The boys turned
away and started back up the corduroy trail toward the
Flat Road and home.

As they passed the schoolhouse, where the women
were still scrubbing up for the opening of school the
next week, two older boys about Theo's age swung down
from a white pine near the road and ran after them.
Theo and Tommy paid no attention, but Herman
turned and watched the boys as they approached.

"Whatcha doin'? Where ya' goin' with the wagon?"
shouted the bigger of the boys.

"Home," said Herman simply.

"Sellin' potatoes?" asked the smaller of the two. They

*"Maybe you'd bette
go back now*

had caught up with Theo and Tommy and were walking beside them.

"Yer Paw can't even build a haystack," scoffed the bigger, and then turned and ran back a few steps. The smaller boy followed quickly.

Tommy's face was dark red with anger as he turned quickly to answer the boys. Theo held his arm and forced him to turn up the road again.

"Come back here, you roughnecks," called a woman from the school steps. She was big and her voice boomed across to the five boys as if she had been standing next to them.

"Yes, Ma," said the two strange boys, and ran back toward the schoolyard.

"Give my respects to your Paw, boys," the woman shouted, "and hope he gits up and around agin soon." She waved in a friendly manner. Theo waved back slowly.

As the strange boys drew away, their backs presented themselves to Herman, who reached down for a large stone and threw it with great accuracy into the middle of the bigger boy's back.

"Now you'll catch it!" yelled Theo as he and Tommy took to their heels. Herman was slowed by the wagon as he clattered up the wooden road, with the enemy close behind. He reached the top of the road, but just as his pursuers slowed and looked as if they might go back, Herman tripped and fell, his cart thumping to a halt against a stone at the side of the road. Tommy and Theo, who had been running slowly just ahead of Herman, heard him fall and stopped. When the two strange boys reached Herman's side, Theo and Tommy stepped up to them. With a menacing look and threatening fists, Theo said, "Maybe you'd better go back now." His voice was low and precise and made the village boys back slowly away and then turn reluctantly down the wooden track into the village.

"All right, get up now," Tommy said to Herman and poked him with his foot.

"Don't ever do that again, not if you can't stay on your feet," said Theo.

Herman said nothing, but getting very slowly to his feet, he looked at his hands. Two or three pieces of gravel had imbedded themselves in his palms. He brushed them off and said nothing. Theo and Tommy walked away. Herman picked up the handle of the cart and followed, keeping always about fifteen feet behind his brothers.

When they reached home, their father praised them for the bargain they had made.

"Well done, lads. You will be good farmers and traders."

Theo smiled and turned red.

"We saw Rev. Brownlow, Father, and he said to give you his best wishes," Tommy said.

"Thank you. A kindly man." Jacob turned to Herman and said, "And what have you been doing, my son? Your clothes are more torn and dirty than usual."

"I fell, Father." Herman looked at the floor and was silent a moment. Theo and Tommy started to speak.

"Papa. . . ."

"Father. . . ."

"I was in a fight," said Herman loudly, interrupting them.

"A fight? I am sorry, my son. Tell me about it." He quickly held up his hand as Theo and Tommy both started to talk.

"Herman, please," he said.

Herman, with a few promptings from Theo, told his story.

"Please. Do not throw rocks. You would be most sorry if you should ever hurt someone that way," said Jacob when his son had finished. Herman looked doubtful. "It is true, you will know it some day, my son." Jacob patted his arm.

The boys went into the large room and put away the precious food they had brought home. Then Theo took the bottle of linament into the bedroom and carefully rubbed his father's back. In the meantime, Herman had taken a lump of sourdough from the bucket down the well, and started to make bread. The sourdough was used in place of yeast and when Herman had made his dough, he would take a piece of it and store it away for use the next time. This way, if he always remembered to save a piece of bread dough, and never let the dough dry out, they would have bread almost forever without having to add more yeast.

Herman sang with great spirit as he mixed and pounded the simple dough. His arms were floury to the elbows when he had finished and set the bread to rise on the hearth. An old flour sack served as an apron and when he had cleaned the table, he shook the sack out the door with a flourish. Before he closed the door on the red sky of evening and the chill wind that blew from across the bay, he waited while Tommy trotted across the yard, expertly swinging the milk pail in time with his walk so that not a drop splashed over the lip.

"Not long till Christmas, is it, Tom?" said Herman.

Tommy laughed.

"Quite a long time. It's only just the first of October. Lookit: most of the birds are still here." The boys listened a moment to the drowsy snippets of conversation

41

among the birds settling for the night in the pines near the house.

"Well, still," said Herman, "it'll snow soon and then it will be Christmas, I know."

"Pooh," said Tommy, but without conviction.

4
A Christmas Secret

In a few weeks, though, the birds were gone. The ice began to pile itself along the beach and the days grew very short.

On the day before Christmas, the wind howled through the trees around the house. The day was almost dark, although it was still early. Snow drove through the air in straight, horizontal lines and Herman's cheeks were raw with its sting as he kicked vigorously at the cabin door, waiting for someone to open it. He carried a full pail of milk in each hand.

"Why were you so long?" he asked as Theo opened the door just enough so that Herman could slip in with his burden.

"I was with Father and I didn't hear you right away. The wind makes so much noise. Where's Tommy?"

"He thought she should have clean straw on Christmas Eve."

Snow drove through the air

"Oh. Yes, she should," Theo said absently. He turned back to the fireplace and a low stool there. He sat down and picked up a knife and a flat piece of wood.

Herman took the milk pails to a small, heavy door in a back corner. He opened it and after covering the milk, put the pails through the door into a low space beyond. This was their cold room; usually, things did not freeze there, but they were kept cold, being shut away from the heat of the room.

"Have you finished yet?" asked Herman.

"No, but I will soon." Theo held up the piece of wood to show, carved deeply into its surface, the figure of an animal.

"What kind of animal is it supposed to be?"

"A goat, of course, stupid. Can't you see that?"

"Humm," said Herman diplomatically. This Tirggel mold had cost Theo many hours of work and the piece of maple he used was smooth and shiny from much handling it during his patient labor. He would give it to his father the next day as the boys' only present to him and tomorrow they would bake the old-fashioned Tirggel cookies formed with the mold.

Herman took off his wraps and hung them on the pegs in the wall near the fireplace. First he unwound a long piece of plaid material from his head. Then he took off his jacket, an old one of his father's too large for him, but pinned and rolled to keep it out of his way as much as possible. Underneath, wrapped around his chest several times, was a knitted scarf of many colors and stitches. His feet and legs were wrapped in rags and bits of old quilting. Over these he wore an unmatched pair of rubbers. Under these were his much-darned socks and when he hung everything on the pegs nearest the fire, he found his shoes on the hearth and put them on. They almost fit and he was very proud of them.

Tommy blew in a few minutes later and stamped and snorted on the doormat for a minute.

"Aren't you almost done, Theo? Tonight is Christmas Eve, you know."

Theo gave Tommy a very dark look and said nothing. Tommy came and looked over his shoulder.

"It's beautiful, Theo," he said enthusiastically, "Papa will be so happy to have it."

Herman said, "Shh," and pointed to the bedroom door, which stood open so that as much of the fire's warmth as possible would reach the sick man lying there.

Tommy clapped his hand over his own mouth and then went to the wall pegs to hang up his wraps.

"Herman," he said sternly, "why is it that your clothes are always nearest the fire?"

"Because I'm colder than anyone else, I guess," murmured Herman, and he huddled closer to the fire.

Tommy removed his outer clothes much as Herman had done, with some differences. His jacket fit him better and he had a real hat, but he did not have rubbers and he had to wear his shoes, wrapped carefully in two pieces of old sail given him by Leander Boyle.

"Boys," came Jacob's voice from the bedroom, "Theodore, Thomas, come here, please."

The two boys, followed by Herman, hurried into the bedroom. Their father was sitting with his legs over the side of the bed.

"Please, get me my trousers, Herman. Theodore and

"It's beautiful, Theo"

Thomas, get on either side of me, please. I am going to sit beside the fire and eat with you this evening. Afterwards, I will tell you the story of Christmas and perhaps we will sing."

"Yes, Father," said the boys in unison and then scurried to help him.

In the other room, Jacob sat on a low chair, wrapped in quilts from his bed. Theo and Herman fixed their plain supper, fish and applesauce tonight, while Tommy stacked more wood beside the fireplace.

After supper, and after the dishes had been washed and dried, Jacob beckoned the boys to sit around him by the hearth.

He had read the simple tale of Jesus' birth so often, over the years, that now, even though his precious books had gone up in smoke, he could recite the story almost without hesitating. The boys listened quietly, Tommy with tears in his eyes, Herman clasping his knees tightly to his chest.

When Jacob had finished, all of them sat still for a few moments while they heard the dying wind in the chimney and the logs in the fireplace sent up showers of sparks.

"Tell about the bells, Papa . . ." began Herman.

". . . and the Christkindli, too," finished Tommy.

"The bells. The bells of Zurich," began Jacob," are not like anything in the whole world. Their sound is so beautiful, so sweet that people come from far away just to hear them on Christmas Eve."

"They don't start together, do they?" prompted Theo, who had heard the story before.

"No, no, they start one at a time, each church bell in the city calling its people to midnight service. Then, on they ring, slowly their melodies meeting, until, finally, they are ringing in a harmony so lovely that it is like a symphony." He paused.

". . . a concert," urged Tommy.

"Yes, a concert." Jacob smiled gently at the boy who had never heard any concert except that of the birds and waves and wind. "The sound fills the valley and echoes from the mountainsides."

"Tell us about the Christkindli, now, Papa."

"Oh, yes, that would interest you most, wouldn't it, little one?" Jacob answered and patted Herman's head.

"Yes, Papa," said Herman shyly.

"Well, he does not come until the day after Christmas in Switzerland, not like St. Nicholas does in this country. No, the Christkindli is very different. The Christkindli is a beautiful angel who drives a sleigh drawn by six tiny reindeer and wears a golden crown. This angel drives through the villages, giving the children gifts."

"Will the Christkindli ever come here, do you think?" asked Herman.

Jacob was silent a moment and then said, "I think someday he might. If we hope and pray."

"And work hard," said Tommy. His father nodded.

The father and his three sons were quiet for a time, looking at the fire and listening to the whisper of the wind in the chimney.

"The wind has died. Look, Theodore, and see if there is much snow."

Theo went to the door and opened it. A few large flakes of snow ventured softly into the cabin as he stood looking out. It was very dark and the sound of Theo's voice was muffled as he said, "It is snowing very hard. By morning, we'll be lucky to get to the barn." He closed the door and turned back to the rosy warmth within.

"Well, three strong boys can shovel a path there, surely," said Jacob and smiled at his sons.

"Now we shall sing a few Christmas hymns and then we should all go to bed."

The four sang well together and they raised their voices heartily in the old hymns they had known since childhood, most of them in a foreign tongue that Herman understood only now and then. When they had finished, Tommy banked the fire and Herman and Theo helped their father back to his bed and made sure he was comfortable.

"Thank you, boys. You are a great comfort to me. I feel that you will not have to take care of me much longer, that very soon I shall again be able to take care of you. Good night, boys."

"Good night, father," said Herman and Theo together.

The boys left the room and waited at the foot of the ladder to the loft while Tommy finished banking the fire, then the three of them climbed together into the loft. The house was very dark.

Their beds were roughly made cornhusk mattresses covered with ticking and several layers of quilts and sacking. Each had molded his bed into the shape that best suited his body and the way he slept.

Usually, they crawled quickly between the covers and then took off the top layer of their clothing. Tonight in the darkness Herman did just that, but Tommy and Theo only pretended they were. They said good night to each other and all three lay still. Finally, Tommy whispered to Theo, "I think he's asleep now." They listened a moment and could hear the quiet breathing of their brother.

When they crawled from under their quilts, the cold

air made them shiver and the mattresses crunched and crackled loudly. Both stopped in alarm, but Herman slept on without stirring. The two boys crept down the ladder.

Theo, with a sigh, pulled on his outdoor clothing and very quietly opening the door, disappeared outside. Tommy, standing on a stool, groped in a narrow space between the chimney and the wall. He pulled out two small, flat, wooden boxes. They were bleached white and smooth and were Tommy's treasures. He had found them on the beach after the spring breakup one year. Many precious things came the boys' way in that fashion.

Tommy was just putting the boxes on the table when Theo pushed open the door and whispered loudly, "Hold the door, Tommy."

Tommy held the door wide while Theo pulled a small spruce tree, two boards nailed crosswise to the bottom of its trunk.

When the tree was in and Tommy had closed the door, the boys carefully set the tree upright. It was about four feet tall, full and bushy and bright green. Tommy sighed.

"It's beautiful, Theo," he whispered.

"It is," said Theo, and took off his wraps.

Tommy opened the wooden boxes and carefully turned over their contents. There were two long chains of dried berries, several irregular pieces of glass, a few pieces of bright paper cut in star and snowflake shapes. Tommy had bored holes in the glass pieces and threaded each with a loop of string. The paper shapes also had string loops. He looked the collection over critically.

"It's too bad we don't have some of the things Mama and Papa brought from Zurich."

50

In the feeble glow of the banked fire

"Well, we don't," said Theo, "and these things are fine. You've done a good job."

Tommy looked pleased and started to drape one of the berry chains around the tree. Theo, too, picked up a chain and began to help decorate the tree. The boys worked quickly and quietly in the feeble glow from the banked fire. When they were done, they stood back and looked solemnly at their handiwork. The coals in the fireplace glinted and sparkled in the glass ornaments, and the paper stars and snowflakes gleamed faintly against the darkness of spruce. The boys smiled and looked at each other with pleasure.

"The snow is very deep," said Theo, "and it's still snowing. I'm glad I thought of putting the tree on the roof. I couldn't have found it, otherwise."

Tommy took his treasured boxes from the table and started up the ladder.

"We'll have to shovel out to the barn in the morning, like Papa says," he said.

Within minutes the two boys had settled themselves in bed and were sound asleep. The snow fell thickly outdoors, and far down near the lake, in Antrim, the small bell on the Baptist church rang quietly over the dunes for midnight services.

When Herman awoke the next morning, he found himself alone in the loft. He could hear his brothers moving about downstairs and his father's voice calling from the bedroom. He reached for his clothes and scrambled into them as best he could under the quilts. When he reached the bottom of the ladder, he turned and saw the tree. His father was sitting beside it and his brothers were standing by his chair.

"What . . ." said Herman, going slowly across the

small room. The fire was roaring and the light danced and glittered on the small tree.

"I think," said Jacob, "that the Christkindli has been here, my son." He held out his hand to Herman and the boy came slowly and dreamily toward him. Holding his father's hand, he knelt before the tree and looked at it in silence.

"Well, do you like it, Herman?" asked Tommy at last.

"It's, well . . . well . . . it's . . . I can hardly believe it," said Herman slowly.

Tommy laughed and danced a little step on the hearth, while Theo smiled broadly and started to put out the plates for breakfast.

For a long time Herman and his father sat hand in hand, looking at the tree. Finally, Herman rose and started to put on his scarves and coat and rubbers. Theo and Tommy looked at him in surprise.

"Where are you going?" asked Tommy

"Out. To dig to the barn, of course."

Theo looked sheepishly at his father.

"Yes, of course."

"Well, son, I guess we all forget now and then."

Herman, dressed at last, opened the door and stepped back quickly as a wave of snow fell in through the door.

"Look!" he shouted and Theo and Tommy ran to his side.

The snow was almost over Herman's head at the doorway. Beyond were white valleys and hills, pierced here and there by small mysterious caverns and hung with miniature cliffs. The moon, setting across the ice-tumbled lake, made every tree an unknown being. The boys giggled and shouted and pushed Herman out and rushed to get their own wraps.

"Here, boys, here!" called Jacob after them, "what about breakfast?" But it was no use; they were gone. After a few minutes Jacob rose slowly from the chair and stood a few moments, finally putting the quilt that had covered him on the back of the chair. Then he moved across the room haltingly, holding the table now and then, but at last moving on his own to the cupboard, where he started to take down eggs and butter. He smiled in triumph.

Outside, the boys had thrown handfuls of snow at each other. In places it reached Theo's shoulders. Finally, each boy found a shovel in the barn, after pushing there through the snow as if it had been the surf. They set to work shoveling a path back to the house. Tommy broke the trail, throwing massive chunks of snow

Widening the path

wildly from the path. Theo followed, widening the path and cutting the sides evenly and precisely. Herman came last, cleaning the way thoroughly.

When they reached the house, they hung the shovels from three nails under the eaves beside the door, then Tommy walked back to the barn, in the moonlit corridor, to milk the cow.

When Theo and Herman found that their father had fixed the breakfast, they looked at each other uneasily, but Jacob said, almost jovially, "Never mind, boys, I shall be able to do more and more as the days go by. And it is best that I do, so that I will be strong enough to help with the planting, when spring comes."

"Yes, Father," said Theo with a happy smile.

Tommy came in with a pail of milk and when he was ready the four sat down together. They bowed their heads as Jacob said a simple grace.

When the meal was almost over, Theo rose suddenly from the table and ran up the loft ladder very quickly. The other three looked surprised for a moment and then Herman said, "Oh!" with an air of remembering, and then Tommy, too, remembered. Their father sat, still puzzled, while Theo clambered down the ladder again, holding a cloth-wrapped parcel in his hand. He walked to the table and slowly handed the package to his father. Jacob smiled at him and unwrapped the piece of clean but faded calico. Inside was the wooden mold that Theo had carved.

"A Tirggel mold!" said Jacob softly and tears welled suddenly in his eyes. "Thank you, my son. Thank you."

"We all did it, Father. Herman found the wood and Tommy cut it to the right size and carved the figure."

"No," said Tommy, "Theo should get the credit.

He did most of the work and he thought it up in the first place."

"I am touched, my boy, and very pleased."

"But how do we make the cookies?" asked Herman.

His brothers and father laughed.

"Of course you'd think of that," said Tommy.

"Well?"

"Tirggel cakes are made of wheat flour and honey," said their father.

"See? I told you!" said Theo triumphantly. He went to the cupboard and took, from the back of the top shelf, a brown crock, covered with oiled paper.

"Herman found a bee tree last summer, and I got some of the honey and saved it, because I thought the Christmas cookies were made with honey."

"A bee tree? How wonderful. I hope you marked it, so that we can go back there again this summer," said Jacob.

"They logged it off," said Tommy matter-of-factly. Herman looked grim and Jacob sighed.

"Our wheat flour is very coarse," said Theo.

"That won't matter," said Jacob. "Tirggel were first made by people who lived many centuries ago, and they did not even have sugar. That is why they are sweetened with honey, so coarse flour should be just the thing. Now, let us clean the breakfast things, sweep the floor, and then Theo can make his cookies . . . so that we will have something to offer our friends, if any should find their way through the snow to visit us today."

For the next few hours the boys worked happily, their father resting again on his bed. Theo made the dough for his cookies and cleared a place among the logs in the fire for the heavy kettle they used as an oven. The kettle could bake only a few cookies at a time, so it was two or three hours before Theo decided he had made enough. When he was through, the three boys washed themselves and brushed and straightened their clothes, hoping there would be company.

When the afternoon was half gone, visitors arrived and several more came before dusk fell. They talked with Jacob and told him how happy they were that he was recovering. Rev. Brownlow arrived with peppermint sticks for each of the boys and Leander Boyle with a slab of smoked fish that he put in Herman's sole charge. The boys made coffee, heavy with chicory as their father liked it, and passed the Tirggel cakes. Two or three children came with their parents and Herman was pleased to discover that they did not have Christmas trees in their houses. This gave Herman the kind of opportunity to brag that did not come his way very often. Theo had to throw him a warning look now and then.

As evening fell and the last of the visitors left, Jacob, who had been sitting by the fire all afternoon, asked to be helped back to bed.

"Are you in pain, Father?" asked Tommy, when his father was settled.

"No, no, son. I am just very tired. I will have my supper in here, if you please."

"Should you get up tomorrow, do you think?" asked Theo.

"Oh, yes. A little every day, and a little more every day, will help me get my strength. Now, hurry and finish boiling the chicken and the potatoes."

Theo and Tommy prepared supper and the four ate in comfortable silence, Herman watching his tree from fairyland.

Jacob went to sleep early and the boys soon followed, climbing the ladder sleepily.

"That was the best Christmas ever," said Herman with a yawn.

"Isn't it always?" said Theo.

"Ummmm," said Tommy.

5
A Bad Accident

Winter softened finally and the sun was already in the sky, glimmering redly behind the eastern forest, as they ate their breakfast. The huge blocks of ice that had piled on the beach during the winter storms were disappearing so quickly that they would be completely gone within a few days. The beach would be left scored with huge pools and long, wide furrows, as if the giant Manitou had walked that way. Kewadin, the great Indian hunter who lived here and there around Torch Lake, had told the boys of Manitou, the Indian spirit.

When at last the ice was gone from the bay, the ships would come again to take away the lumber cut during the winter. Tommy shouted a great halloo at the thought and skipped a giant step as he ran through the slushy snow toward the barn, the milk pail swinging violently beside him. His greatest ambition was to work on the beach, helping to load the ships, and he loved to watch the slow, stately operation.

The trees looked curiously fat and rosy. The pale sunlight gleamed on wet branches. A bundle of wet snow left the eaves, quite suddenly, as Tommy banged open the low barn door.

As he milked the brown and white cow, he talked to her softly, telling her about the beach and the perfect little poplars that grew along the bottom of the bluff and up its scarred and ruined sides, how soon their dancing leaves would reflect the shimmer of the sun on the waves of the bay. The cow listened for word of the green upland meadows.

When he had finished the milking and had cleaned the cow's stall and had given her new feed, he went back to the house, with great splashing.

"Well, I think spring is coming at last," Tommy shouted as he entered the house.

Herman was kneading bread at the table. Theo and his father were looking at two axes, which they held up to the little window for better light. All of them turned and smiled at Tommy.

"In this land, Thomas," said his father, "even the end of March is too early for saying that." He bent over the axe blade again.

"Well, it feels like it to me," said Tommy, a satisfied smile still on his face.

"I know," said Theo with sympathy, "even if it snows tomorrow, it will be a spring snow."

"There," said Herman, and held up high a neat loaf shaped on a flat tin. "And I remembered the salt today."

"Well, boys," said Jacob, walking across the room to the door, "today we will look at trees and perhaps fell a few, to start clearing south of the potato field. Herman, you stay here and sweep and bring in wood until the bread has risen again and you can bake it. I don't want it all over the hearth, as happened last week."

"Yes, Papa," said Herman with great disappointment in his voice.

"Don't fret," whispered Tommy as he followed his father and Theo out the door, "this afternoon we'll go down to the beach and look for shipwrecks." Many ships went down on Lake Michigan, particularly in the fall, and by spring the boys could find the debris of these tragedies scattered along the beach: giant pulleys, tin bread boxes, now and then part of a chair, a bottle, even a small skiff, oarless but watertight.

Herman brightened and picked up the broom.

Tommy ran splashing after his father and brother.

When they reached the far side of the potato field, their father pointed to a birch tree standing only a little way from the edge of the field, at one side of a small cluster of trees.

"Let's start there, boys," said their father.

61

Theo swung the axe down from his shoulder and started toward the tree.

"You're a better woodsman than your brother, Thomas," said Jacob quietly, "so you work with him on this tree."

"Yes, Papa," said Tommy proudly and walked toward the tree also.

For several minutes the sounds of the chopping echoed and rang through the little woods. Jacob had walked farther into the clump of trees and presently returned. The boys rested their axes a minute and Jacob said,

"Fine, boys, but when it's down, please call me so that I can limb out."

"Yes, Papa," said Theo. Tommy merely swung his axe up and started to chop again.

In a few more minutes, the tree started to crack and pop at the place where the boys had been cutting. Both jumped quickly away and watched the tree begin to fall, very slowly at first and then more quickly. Before it reached the ground, the boys saw that it was going to catch in a nearby tree. The cut end of the trunk rolled wildly on the stump for a few seconds and then slid to a precarious stop, still atop the stump.

Tommy ran back to the fallen tree. He hefted his axe for a moment and started to whack at the nearest limb.

"Tom! Father said to let him do that!" shouted Theo.

"It's all right," said Tommy gruffly, "he meant you, not me."

"What are you saying!" said Theo, "he meant both of us. Stop! Do you hear me?"

Tommy went ahead slashing at the limb. The leaves that trailed from it to the ground danced crazily with each blow. There was a sharp splintering sound and the limb bounced to the ground. Tommy looked a moment at his work with great satisfaction. Theo ran up to him.

"You fool!" he cried, "why don't you wait for Father as he said?"

"I'm all right. Leave me alone."

Tommy picked up his axe and, tramping around to the other side of the tree, started to chop at another limb. This time the limb stayed very still, not bouncing at all. It felt firm and solid beneath the blows of his axe. Tommy worked quickly and with a look of great self-satisfaction on his face. Theo stood nearby for a moment and then, standing his own axe against a tree, ran through the woods calling, "Father! Father!" Tommy snorted with irritation but did not look up.

Soon his axe had bitten through the limb, but still the limb did not fall. Tommy pushed at it with his foot and heard the familiar splintering. He looked puzzled as the branch still did not move. A squeaky crash sounded behind him and he turned quickly, but not in time to step from the path of the tree trunk as it rolled from the stump.

Tommy went down beneath the tree and gave a short scream as the whole tree bounced and floundered and resettled itself. The heavy trunk was on his leg and Tommy started to cry out again as he felt a strong long snap in his leg. He could not hear the snap amid the crashings of the tree, but he felt its loudness quiver along his leg and up through his body. He drew a quick, deep breath and then let it out as if he were strangling.

"Tommy! Tommy!" he heard his father calling as he ran with Theo through the woods.

"Tommy, are you hurt?" he asked as he knelt beside the boy.

Tommy could not answer, but nodded his head once.

"Theo, quick, help me lift the tree from his leg," said Jacob.

The tree was solid and heavy, its slippery bark hard to grasp. The man and boy strained for what seemed like ages and finally, with a huge effort, flung the trunk away. Still the leg hurt. Tommy looked at it only a second and then closed his eyes, his stomach churning.

"I will carry him, Theo. Run ahead and see that my bed is fixed for him." Theo ran silently away, across the potato field.

"Tommy, lad, can you put your arms around my neck?" Tommy lifted his arms gingerly and almost cried out before he had reached his father's neck.

"I will help you. Grit your teeth hard, my son." Jacob bent above the boy and, gently lifting Tommy's arms, helped the boy grasp his neck. Then, sliding his arms as gently as he could under Tommy's sturdy thighs and shoulders, he struggled to his feet, jerking a little with his burden, and feeling in his arms the tautness of agony in his son's body.

As he walked swiftly across the muddy potato field, he met Theo returning at a run.

"The bed will be ready, Papa. What should I do now?"

"Go into Antrim and get Dr. Belliger."

"But, Papa . . ." began Theo.

"Go. Do as I say."

"Yes, Papa," said Theo, preparing to hurry away again. Theo looked down at Tommy's leg.

"Hurry, Son, hurry"

"Papa! Look!" His voice was a scream.

Jacob shifted his eyes for a moment to his son's legs. He winced and hurried on. Bright blood was dripping from the toes of Tommy's shoes.

"Hurry, son! Hurry!"

6
Theo Finds a Doctor

It was a long run to the village. Theo stumbled in the muddy road now and then. In the deep shade patches of snow were treacherously slippery. Twice, but only twice, he leaned against a tree and, sobbing, gasped until he caught his breath. Leander waved in greeting as Theo passed his cabin, but the boy barely saw him. On and on he ran. At last, off the Flat Road, his heels pounded hard on the logs of the road leading down into Antrim.

The street was deserted, he saw, as he turned around the last sandy hill. Two horses, one hitched to a farm wagon, stood restlessly in front of Mrs. Webster's boarding house, halfway down to the pier. The long pier, empty too, stretched its beseeching finger into the bay where sand-covered ice floes jostled in the sun-sparkled water.

His heels pounded hard

Theo stopped only a second in front of the feed store and then turned into the covered stairway that ran up the side of the building. Two steps at a time he ran, and fell on his hands at the top, only to jump up again and rush panting into the room at the top.

"Doctor . . . Doctor!" he panted, "Doctor Belliger, you've got . . . you're . . . the only. . . . Come, come! It's Tommy!"

A youngish man in a neat, grey jacket, who had been sitting with a book beside the open front window, took one stride to Theo and, concern in his face, said,

"What is it, lad? Tell me. Here, take a breath first and sit down. Calm, calm yourself." As he spoke, he led Theo to the chair by the window and pushed him gently down.

"No . . . no, Doctor," said Theo, rising again, "there's no time, it's Tommy . . . his leg."

"His leg? said the doctor uncertainly.

"Yes," said Theo, and filled his chest with air and then spoke strongly.

"You're the only one who can help. Tommy's broken his leg and Dr. Ingoldsby is a day's ride away in Elk Rapids. You got to come!" He pulled at the doctor's arm.

"But a leg," said the doctor, not taking his arm away from Theo's urgent hands. "I'm a dentist, son . . . what is your name? You're one of the Germans, aren't you? What's the name? Escher?"

"Swiss, sir, and I'm Theo. Come, please. He's bleeding!"

They stood close together, very still for a moment, the doctor looking with a frown into the streaked, agony-laden younger face before him.

"I'll come," he said finally, and went swiftly to a cupboard. "I've no anesthetic," he said, almost to himself, "it'll be hard."

He found a leather case in a drawer and began filling it with antiseptic, bright scissors, and thin, small knives.

"Have you anything we can use as bandages?" he asked.

Theo thought for a moment, his fists clenched in front of him. "No, nothing," he said finally.

Without a word the doctor opened a drawer and took out two large, white, apronlike things with metal eyelets in two corners. He folded them and stuffed them into the small case.

He turned and grabbed Theo by the arm, hurrying him out of the room and down the stairs.

"I don't have a horse," the doctor said belligerently.

"Neither do we," said Theo.

The pair started walking swiftly up the sandy road. The doctor walked steadily and with wide strong strides, but Theo kept urging him, with short running steps now and then, to go more quickly. But the doctor's face was set and grim and every so often he looked at Theo and held him back with his long, very clean hand. Finally, they settled into a steady, marching walk. For a while, neither said anything, then the doctor spoke. "How did it happen, Theo?"

"We were cutting down a tree and when Tommy started to limb out, it fell and the trunk smashed his leg." Theo sniffed and jammed his hand in his pockets.

"Pretty bad, hummm," said the doctor softly.

"Yes. Lots of blood and . . . and. . . ." Theo gritted his teeth.

"That's all right, you don't have to talk about it."

The doctor stopped suddenly.

"We'll need help to set the leg. Two men, at least," he said. "There! There's Jake Masterson! Jake! Jake!" called Dr. Belliger. The tall figure, walking slowly toward the boarding house, stopped and turned toward them.

"Whatcha' want, Doc?"

"We need you, Jake, t' help set a broken leg."

Jake came to where they stood.

"Well, all right, I guess. Be back by noon, tho'."

Dr. Belliger did not answer but started again walking up the log trail. Jake fell in behind, Theo still slightly ahead.

They walked in silence until they came to Leander's cabin. Dr. Belliger stopped and called loudly.

"Leander! Leander Boyle!"

Leander put his head out of the door.

"Whatcha' want?"

"Help set a broken leg!"

Leander disappeared without a word and a moment later stepped into the sunshine, pulling on an old jacket.

Leander joined Jake and the small procession went on up the Flat Road. They reached the farm without stopping again and Theo pushed open the door for the men.

The sun was high in the sky now, but the inside of the small cabin was dark and gloomy. The fire had almost gone out and Herman was kneeling on the hearth laying sticks across the grate with shaking hands. He thrust a handful of soft dry grass into the small pile of smoking coals and waited while it flared and licked at the kindling.

"Doctor, thank God you have come!" Jacob stepped from the bedroom and indicated that the doctor was to follow him there.

"Here he is. It is very bad. Help him."

"I'll see. I'm just a dentist, but I'll try to help," the doctor muttered as he took off his coat and threw it into the corner of the room. Jake slipped hesitantly into the room, but Leander shouldered him aside and stood close to the doctor's side.

Tommy was laid carefully on the bed, his crumpled, bleeding leg stripped bare and resting on a folded quilt. His head was thrown back and pushed deeply into the pillow. On either side of him, his hands clutched great handfuls of the blankets, his knuckles white. Now and then a gasping sob came from deep within him, and from his eyes tears poured, although he did not cry aloud.

Dr. Bellinger looked down at him a moment and then bent over the injured leg. The leg was scraped and raw and halfway down to the ankle was a dark, open wound, on the inside of the calf. Through it glistened the grayish white end of the bone. He shook his head and made subdued whistling breaths with his tongue.

"You must know, Mr. Escher," said the doctor, "that I have no anesthetic, and that it will be very difficult for the boy and that, in addition, I am a dentist and whatever I do today must be seen as soon as possible by a medical doctor."

"I understand, I understand, but you were our only hope. Help us," pleaded Jacob.

"I will. Heat some water, find me two boards as long as his leg and wrap them in blankets. And then tear up these bibs," he said, pulling the white aprons out of his bag and nodding at Herman, who now stood trembling beside the door. When he had issued his orders, Herman turned quickly and went back to the fireplace. Theo took the apronlike bibs in his strong hands and started to tear them into strips.

Jacob held Tommy gently by the shoulders and whispered to him.

"This will hurt, my son. Be brave and pray. I will hold you and help you as much as I can."

"Yes, yes . . ." Tommy sobbed through his teeth, his eyes pinched tightly shut.

When Theo finished tearing the strips of bandage, he stepped out of the room for a moment and soon came back with two flat boards, which he measured hesitantly against Tommy's uninjured leg. They seemed to be the right length. After he had wrapped them in pieces of blanket, he looked around for a place to put them. The doctor saw him and took them with a gentle smile and leaned the boards against the end of the bed.

"You, Jake, hold him on one side, Leander on the other. Put your arms around his body; don't just pull on his arms." The two men moved into place. "Now, Mr. Escher, you come here. I'll need your help at this end. It will need a great deal of hard pulling to get the bone ends together. Get yourselves in place. I want to look at it first." He bent over Tommy's leg again.

"I am a dentist"

"Both bones, I'm sure," he muttered.

Then he placed the padded boards, one on each side of the leg, on the bed. He wrapped one of the strips around Tommy's foot, trying hard not to move the leg. Tommy moaned and panted, sweat pouring from his face.

The doctor picked up two ends that he had left dangling from the bandage on Tommy's foot. He tied them firmly together, leaving a loop. He fitted his right hand into this loop and settled it fussily. Then he pulled his hand out, quickly, and thrust his left hand into the loop. When he had finally settled his left hand, he spoke.

"Now, I am going to have to pull his leg very hard. You men, as I said, must pull as hard as you can in the other direction. And Mr. Escher, you keep him from slipping. Theo, go help your brother get that water." He paused. "It will hurt a great deal. Now." Theo left the room, very slowly.

Tommy screamed

Bracing his leg against the end of the bed, the doctor gave a strong, steady pull on the bandage. His young muscles strained in the sleeves of his shirt and his hands, strengthened from pulling stubborn molars, whitened with the effort. There was a small grating noise and a tiny slurp in the wound and Tommy screamed.

Doctor Belliger, holding the leg taut, felt at the wound and around it as gently as he could. Tommy screamed, breathlessly this time and with his teeth clenched. His father held him tightly.

"All right, Jake and Leander, let go very slowly when I give the signal. All right. Now." The two men eased their hold on Tommy's body. Tommy sobbed twice.

In the kitchen, Herman huddled beside the fire, now burning well. Streams of tears poured from his eyes, sobs shivered through his chest, but he made no sound. Theo quietly hung a kettle of water over the flames.

"I don't know," said the doctor in the bedroom. "I'm

not sure, but it will help until the doctor comes." He stopped his probing and swabbed the wound gently with peroxide. Tommy's indrawn breath was weary. Jacob still held him close as he watched the doctor worriedly. Several times he started to speak. Then he blurted out, "Thank you, doctor. We haven't much, but we will pay you, do not fear."

The doctor laughed a short laugh.

"Don't thank me yet, and as for pay, why, I'll send a bill sometime, I guess. . . ." He finished dressing the wound and, carefully pressing the padded boards on either side of the wounded leg, tied them very tightly against Tommy's leg with strips of the torn apron.

"He must be absolutely still, Mr. Escher." He rolled down his sleeves and searched a moment through the small leather case. "Here," he went on, "give him one of these powders every three hours. They will help the pain, tho' not as much as I'd like. What I have for toothache won't quite work for a broken leg, I'm afraid." Jacob took the powders.

Theo came into the room.

"Oh, yes, Mr. Escher," the doctor went on, "you keep him warm. If you have an apple crate you can spare, cut out the ends and put it upside down over Tommy's leg and cover it with blankets. He *must* be kept warm."

"Yes, Doctor," said Jacob. "Here, Theo, put this in some water and help Tommy take it, please." Theo ran out of the room with the small white envelope his father had handed him.

Jacob turned to the bed and, being very careful not to disturb the broken leg, covered the rest of his son's body with blankets and quilts.

Jake, who was looking a little pale, and Leander were

still standing near the head of the bed. Jacob turned to them.

"Thank you, thank you both for your kindness." He shook each man by the hand. They nodded and Jake left the room quickly.

". . . gotta git back," he muttered.

Leander stood a moment beside Jacob, looking at the boy on the bed.

The doctor looked at his hands, after he had fastened his cuffs, and said, "I'd better wash." He went quickly into the kitchen, but stopped a second when he saw Herman and said to him, "Come along, boy, and draw some water for me."

He spoke lightly and Herman turned very slowly, his tears stopping, to look at Dr. Belliger.

"It's all over," said the doctor. "He's all right. Now, come and draw some water." He went out the door and waited while Herman rose slowly from his corner and followed him out, wiping his nose on his sleeve and sniffing greatly.

The doctor smiled. He put his arm around Herman's shoulders and together they stepped into the dripping, sunlit farmyard.

7
Sunnyside! Hooray!

For almost two weeks, Tommy lay on the big bed in his father's room. He heard the snow sliding from the roof. He saw the storms come again and the great snowflakes darken the tiny window. Then the sun again, and the rain. Through his pain he knew that spring was coming very fast.

"Ol' Leander'll be waiting for the boat whistle," he whispered to Herman one day, as Herman sat by the bed mending an old moccasin.

"Yup," said Herman, "but he'll have to wait a while longer. 'Cause the ice ain't out at the straits yet." He spoke with importance.

"What do you know, stupid?" said Theo, coming in just then.

"Well," said Herman hurriedly, "I heard about it yesterday when I went to the beach to look for stuff."

"What did you find?" asked Tommy in his weak voice.

"Nothing," said Herman disgustedly, "nothing but junk."

"Well," said Theo, "that's all we ever find, isn't it?"

Tommy turned his head slowly.

"What's the matter, Theo?" he said, "you're so grumpy."

"Oh, oh, nothing." Theo stomped out of the room.

"What is it, Herman, what is it?"

"Oh, we just wonder when the doctor is going to get here."

"I'll be all right," said Tommy, and weakly turned his head toward the window.

Just then they heard, clear but far away, a long, sharp whistle. Both boys stayed rigidly still and listened again. Again it came, longer this time, although still clear and distant.

"It's the *Sunnyside*!" screamed Herman and threw the moccasin across the room.

Tommy beat gently, but with fierce joy, on the quilts that covered him.

Theo burst into the room.

"The *Sunnyside*!" he shouted.

"Go tell Papa, Herman!" ordered Theo.

"Oh, he heard it," said Herman, "let's go to town and get the doctor!"

"What if he isn't on the boat?" said Theo with apprehension.

"He'll be there," said Herman. "Dr. Belliger said he'd be on it." Herman admired Dr. Belliger and knew the young dentist would not disappoint them.

"Go find out," murmured Tommy from the bed.

"We will, we will, Tom. Just lie still," said Theo.

Herman and Theo left the room and hurried across

the farmyard to the barn, but before they reached it, they met their father coming out with a leather pail that had held scraps for their few chickens.

"You heard it, boys?" he called.

"Yes, Papa, can we go into Antrim to meet it?"

"Yes, yes, run along. Herman, stay with Theo, and don't have any more disagreements with your friends in town." He spoke sternly, but smiled into Herman's small intense face.

Herman said, "Yes, Papa," and darted after Theo, who had already started toward the Flat Road.

Spring had truly come to much of the forest land, and near the road trillium and snowdrops thrust up from the leaf mold and the dead grasses. The hump between the wagon ruts had dried and this was where they walked. Once they passed a logger driving two huge horses that dragged two hemlocks behind them. He waved his peavy at the boys.

"You men goin' to load the *Sunnyside,* huh?" He laughed loudly at his own joke and gave a whistling crack of his whip over the horses' heads and burst into song as the boys smiled and walked on.

"I could, you know, I could," muttered Theo when they were well away from the man.

"Of course you could. So could Tommy, if he didn't have a broken leg," said Herman loyally.

When they drew nearer Antrim, they began to hear distant shouts and the jumbled rattling of a wagon being driven very fast. When finally they rounded the dune and looked down into Antrim's main street, they could see the crowds gathered at the end of the pier. Almost docked now at the far end of the long pier was the *Sunnyside.*

She was not a large steamship and she was able to

come right to the end of the Antrim pier. Many boats of deeper draft had to anchor out a ways in the shallow harbor and lighter their cargoes back and forth. On the forward deck of the *Sunnyside,* just in front of the wheelhouse, was a curious little six-sided building with a top like a Chinese pagoda. Even her captain couldn't explain why his ship, otherwise so plain and straight-forward, should have such an exotic structure. Perhaps some homesick Chinese laborer had been left alone

working on her deck for a day. Her broad, rounded bottom was now dented and scratched from pushing her way through chunks of ice in harbors farther north. A sailor made the long, daring leap from her deck to the pier and turned in time to catch a rope snaked through the air by a sailor on deck. In a few minutes she would be berthed.

The Sunnyside *gave a firm, final blast*

The crowd was spread out down the long pier. At
the land end women and girls stood talking together in
small groups, not many actually stepping onto the pier
itself. At the end near the ship stood the men and boys.
A few of the girls had ventured to the very back fringes
of this crowd, and Theo and Herman pushed themselves
through with a businesslike air of importance. Other
boys had also pushed their way through to the front of
the crowd and Theo and Herman joined a small group
behind the front row of important town officials.

Supervisor McDavitt was still pulling on his coat as
he pushed through the crowd to the front row. As he
reached his place, he straightened his tie and gave a
final tap to the top of his tall beaver hat. He stood

proudly for a minute or two and then the postmaster, Jeremy Mitchel, tapped his arm and gestured toward Mr. McDavitt's legs. The supervisor looked down crossly and with a sudden blush saw that he still wore the white apron that covered him when he waited on customers in the butcher shop. He fumbled hurriedly under the tails of his coat, untied the apron strings, and snatched it off. He rolled the apron into a ball and looked around frantically for a place to put it. Looking down behind him he saw Herman's intent brown face.

"Here, sonny, take this to my store and there's a nickel in it for you."

Herman looked blank for only a moment and then snatching the white ball, he raced toward the town, his heels pounding on the timbers of the pier. When he reached the feed store, he almost ran into Dr. Belliger, coming down the stairs.

"Hey, Herman, where are you going in such a hurry? The wrong way, too!" called the doctor.

Herman gasped something unintelligible and flung himself into the butcher shop next door. He slapped the apron on the nearest counter and turned back through the door before he came to halt. Arms and legs flying, he passed Dr. Belliger again and waved grimly as he did so.

Herman reached his place again, and tugged at Mr. McDavitt's sleeve. Mr. McDavitt, frowning again, looked down. Then he smiled at Herman and said,

"Get it delivered, boy? Good. Here is your pay," and he handed Herman a silver coin.

"Thank you, thank you," muttered Herman and standing with it in his fist a moment looked up at Theo.

"Be sure there's no hole in the pocket you put it in," said Theo.

"How could there be," asked Herman, puzzled, "I've never used them before. At least, not for money," he added. The vision of several linty frogs and sand-covered clam shells crossed his mind. He stuffed the precious coin into one of the vast pockets of his large-sized trousers. He made sure it nestled safely in the firm bottom, among the twigs and pebbles there.

The *Sunnyside* gave a firm, final blast on its whistle as the gangplank hit the pier. A tall, trim man in a blue uniform started down the gangplank, following a sailor who ran to the bottom and caught several small satchels thrown from the deck. The man in uniform was Captain Duncan. He walked forward and shook Mr. McDavitt's hand.

"Good to see you, Mac. We'll be blowing the horn for logs tomorrow. Hope you're all ready." This last he said to the crowd around him. A lighthearted shout went up from the men and young boys. A hopeful murmur went up from the women in the back. This would mean meat on some tables that had been all but bare for many weeks now.

He turned back to the beaming supervisor.

"We got a Dr. Ingoldsby on board. Said Dr. Belliger sent for him from Traverse City. Here he comes now." The captain turned as a tall, gray-haired man in a stern black suit came down the gangplank. Dr. Belliger stepped forward, his hand out.

"Dr. Belliger? How do you do," said Dr. Ingoldsby, as he shook the younger man's hand.

"How do you do, Dr. Ingoldsby," said Dr. Belliger. "I'm so glad you've come. The patient is a son of Jacob Escher."

Herman and Theo had by this time pushed almost

to the front of the crowd. Theo cleared his throat loudly and Dr. Belliger noticed him.

"Here are his brothers. Herman and Theo, step up and meet Dr. Ingoldsby."

Everyone was watching now, and Mr. McDavitt patted Herman on the shoulder. Theo shook hands seriously.

"It's Tommy, sir," he said. "He broke his leg. It's bad."

"Yes, we should get out there as soon as possible, Doctor," said Dr. Belliger. "I set it as best I could, but I'm afraid it's not going to knit properly."

"Well, let's find a couple of strong men then, Doctor, and be on our way," said Dr. Ingoldsby. He grabbed a black bag from among the satchels on the pier and started off briskly, pushing a path through the crowd, Dr. Belliger, Herman, and Theo trailing after him.

Dr. Ingoldsby gestured at the crowd and said,

"Whatcha want, Doc?"

"Who'd you think'd be good, Dr. Belliger? Hurry, man, there's no time to lose."

Herman wondered at the hurry. It had been eleven days since the accident.

Dr. Belliger stopped by Silas Young, who was in the back of the crowd.

"Will you come, Silas?"

"Shore, Doc, long's we're back by tomorrow." He laughed at his own little joke.

"We'll get Leander on our way out. He's sure to be there."

"Lead the way, lads," said Dr. Ingoldsby.

Herman and Theo walked on ahead, up the road leading through the dunes to the Flat Road. The thaw was in full force now and the woods seemed to run with the sound of water.

The doctors talked quietly and seriously, followed by Silas and led by Herman and Theo. Their boots sucked in the sandy road and sometimes, in a densely shaded spot, crunched through old snow.

When they reached Leander Boyle's house, Dr. Belliger stopped in the road and looked distastefully at the churned and messy mixture of mud and leaves that lay in the path to the cabin. He cupped his hands around his mouth and shouted.

"Leander Boyle!" he called, "Leander! If you're home, come on out." He waited a second or two and was about to call again when the door to the cabin opened with a good deal of squeaking and scraping.

"Whatcha' want, Doc? More bones?" Leander laughed.

"That's right, Leander. Can you spare us half an hour or so?"

"You serious, Doc? That boy break another leg?" The old man looked puzzled now.

"No, Leander, same leg. That is, we got to do it all over again, probably."

"Oh. Yep, I'll come. Just a minute." Leander turned back into his cabin without shutting the door. Two grey cats sidled cautiously in through the open door. As Leander came out again, he kicked the two cats out before him. They ran complaining around the end of the house.

The small procession started up the road again. Silas and Leander walked silently behind the two doctors, trying to hear what they were saying.

Theo and Herman walked in front of the doctors, their ears open wide also.

When they reached the Escher's farmyard, Jacob was waiting by the road. He stepped up to Dr. Ingoldsby.

"Dr. Ingoldsby, I am Jacob Escher, Thomas's father. We are most grateful that you have come and you shall be paid as promptly as we can."

"How do you do, Mr. Escher. I hope I can help your boy. We shall talk about my fee when I know how well I can help him." The two men shook hands and smiled at each other with mutual respect.

When they reached Tommy's bedside, Dr. Ingoldsby spoke a few words to the boy and then took a tape measure from his bag. Leander and Silas stood silently in the doorway, while Jacob and Dr. Belliger watched quietly from the end of the bed. Herman held tightly to Theo's arm as they stood behind the two men in the doorway.

Dr. Ingoldsby, murmuring occasionally to himself, measured both of Tommy's legs very carefully. He looked closely at the splint and the bandages and then faced the little group.

"It was not badly done the first time, but it will have

to be done again. One leg is shorter than the other. We must not let this fine boy grow up a cripple." He turned back to the bed and started to remove his coat.

"Here, you men know what to do." Leander and Jacob nodded, while Dr. Belliger and Silas stepped hastily up to Dr. Ingoldsby's side.

Dr. Ingoldsby stopped and looked at Herman and Theo standing just outside the door in the other room.

"Run along, boys. You can do nothing here." His voice was gentle.

Theo's eyes filled with tears and as he steered Herman out the cabin door with one hand, his other hand was clenched tightly, the knuckles white.

The boys sloshed slowly across the farmyard toward the small barn. Within they could hear the cow stamping and snorting now and then.

"She'd like to be out to pasture," said Herman.

"I think you're right. Say, why don't we go up to the pasture and see how it is. Then, maybe later, if Papa says it's all right, we could take her up there. The snow's gone for this year, for sure."

"Well, all right," Herman began. Just then they heard a scream from the cabin and they turned toward it with pain on their faces.

"Oh, Theo. . . ."

"Don't, Herman. Dr. Ingoldsby's a good man, he won't hurt Tommy any more than he has to, you can tell that."

"Let's go up to the pasture, Theo. Hurry. No . . . no, maybe we should stay here. . . ." Herman ran ahead a few steps and then back, clutching Theo's arm.

"Herman, stop! He'll be all right. . . ." Another scream from the cabin. "Come on, we're going up to the pasture." Theo took Herman firmly by the hand and the two boys marched quickly through the mud and over the flattened brown grass to the foot of the hill. They stopped there a moment and looked back toward the house.

"He'll be all right," said Theo and smiled at Herman.

8
Tommy Walks Again

When Dr. Ingoldsby and the two men had left, walking along the Flat Road, Herman and Theo in the upper pasture saw them and came hesitatingly down to the cabin.

"Papa?" called Theo very softly as he entered the quiet house.

"In here, son," Jacob answered softly from the bedroom.

The boys found Tommy sleeping in exhaustion, his face still stained with tears. Jacob stood beside the bed with a long piece of rope in his hands.

"Walk very softly, boys. The leg must not be jarred at all."

"What are you going to do with the rope, Papa?" asked Herman.

"I am seeing how I can attach it to the ceiling to make

a sling for Thomas's leg so that it will not be bounced
at all."

Tommy stirred on the bed and moaned, but did not
waken.

"We should make a sling and fasten it to one end of
the rope and pass the rope through a loop in the ceiling
and then down to the wall where we can fasten it," Theo
suggested.

"But I must exercise the leg at the knee each day, so I
must be able to lower the sling," said Jacob doubtfully.

"Well, we won't fasten it then, we'll just wind it
around two nails. I've seen something like it when they
load ships at the pier," answered Theo.

"Very good, my son," said Jacob.

By the time Tommy wakened, the sling was fixed and
his leg carefully suspended a little way off the bed.

"He said I'd make a good soldier," whispered Tommy,
as Theo worked fastening the rope to the wall.

"You would. And he should know," said Theo, "He
was at Gettysburg, you know."

"Ummm," murmured Tommy, as he drifted off again.

"It will be bad tonight, I fear," said Jacob. "His feeling is numb now, but in a little while it will return and
the pain will be bad."

"He will bear it, Father, and we must help him," said
Theo.

"Yes, Papa, he is a good soldier," said Herman.

Jacob looked doubtfully at his sons.

The pain did come back that night, and Tommy lay
in anguish while his father and Theo took turns holding
his hand and talking to him. Near dawn Tommy drifted
into a heavy sleep and Jacob, shaking with weariness,
stretched out on a pallet beside the bed. Theo slept in
front of the fire, wrapped in a shabby quilt.

During the long weeks that followed, Herman and Theo shouldered Tommy's chores as well as their own and did all they could to make Jacob's work easier. Tommy suffered pain from his leg, but seeing his father work harder than he should caused him suffering in his mind and heart also. He feared for his father's back.

That spring was hot. Weeds grew faster than ever between the wavering rows of turnips that Herman had planted and all through the stumpy, half-grown corn Theo and his father had sown so laboriously.

"Why should the weeds grow so well and the corn so poorly?" said Jacob with exasperation, as he and Theo stood looking at their crop one day.

"I don't know, Father, but Leander says that the land is not right when it's been logged off."

"What do you mean?" Jacob mopped his neck and face with a large red handkerchief.

"Well, the kinds of trees that grow here take things from the ground and leave nothing for the crops that come after."

"Nonsense! He is a fisherman. What can he know?" He picked up two hoes and handed one to Theo. "We must work harder."

After the noon meal, Jacob went in to exercise Tommy's knee. The boy spoke to him anxiously.

"Father, how much longer will it be? Until I can walk, I mean."

"Well, let's see." Jacob was silent a moment while he began to bend the knee of the injured leg very gently. "You broke your leg at the end of March. It is now June. I would think that in a week or so we could begin to give you more exercise and then by the end of August, surely, you will walk again."

91

"Well, it's not such a long time," said Tommy with a sigh.

"No, indeed," said Jacob.

"Father."

"Yes, son?"

"I worry that you will hurt your back again."

"Ho! I am fine. No need to worry about me."

Tommy did worry, though. During the long spring days and far into the summer he lay, half suspended in the tiny bedroom. Theo and Herman, busy with the season's work, could come in to see him only at meal-times and in the evenings. The summer evenings seemed to last forever for Tommy. His family talked to him and his father told stories, but always, while the sun was still over the horizon, Herman's head would nod and soon he would be asleep, leaning against the side of Tommy's bed. Theo yawned so often and so widely that Tommy sometimes felt he might swallow the room whole. Jacob tried to keep the times happy and lively, but he, too, was weary and usually fell silent while the sky was still pink and yellow from the just-vanished sun.

Some days were exciting for the boy in the itching bandages, but there were not enough of them. Rev. Brownlow visited as often as he could. He admired the small, struggling family and held the boys in great respect.

"Tommy! Tommy!" shouted Herman one day.

He ran into the bedroom and stood panting beside Tommy's bed.

"What is it?" asked Tommy.

"Rev. Brownlow is coming! He's halfway here from Leander's!"

"Oh," said Tommy. "Here, Herman, quick, straighten the quilt!"

Herman gave two huge tugs to the sides of the quilt and then ran to the tiny window that faced toward the road.

"Can you see him? Can you?" said Tommy, smoothing the quilt more gently.

"Now I can!" shouted Herman after a minute.

"Well, go meet him at the road, stupid," said Tommy.

"Yes, I will, I will!" said Herman, grinning as he raced from the room.

Rev. Brownlow came into the room a few minutes later, his arms full of things.

"How are you today, Thomas?" he asked heartily.

"Fine, sir, fine," answered Tommy. Herman hovered in the background, his bare feet dancing very slightly on the rough floor.

"I've brought some things that might interest you."

"Thank you, sir."

"Well," laughed Rev. Brownlow, "don't thank me until you've seen what they are. I know some boys that would be very unhappy with some of the things here." He put his bundles on the floor and lowered himself to the chair that stood beside the bed.

"Let's see. First of all, here's something you might never have seen before." He handed Tommy an orange.

"Oh, thank you, sir!" said Tommy breathlessly. "I saw one once, at Christmas time, when I was a little boy." Herman came closer, very softly and looked at the round object Tommy held.

"I wish I had more, Herman," said Rev. Brownlow regretfully, "but this is the only one I could get."

"Yes, sir," said Herman, still eyeing the fruit.

"Oranges are very good for the health, I am told, and

I thought it might help you build your strength up again."

"When should I eat it?"

"Soon, I should think, or it will spoil. And don't forget to take off the skin," Rev. Brownlow said gravely, and turned to the pile beside him.

"And here is a slate and some chalk."

"Thank you, sir," said Tommy.

"And here, my boy, is a primer. Perhaps your father could take a little while some evening and help you learn the letters. Then, during the day, you could begin to learn reading."

The new pier was coming along we

"Oh, Rev. Brownlow, thank you, sir. Thank you!" Tommy took the small book very gently and looked for a long time at its dingy red cover.

"You can use the slate and the chalk to practice writing the letters you learn."

"Yes, sir." Tommy's voice was very far away and his shining eyes were still on the book in his hands. The orange, which he had put beside him on the bed, started to roll, very slowly, toward the edge. Herman caught it reverently and put it firmly beside his brother again.

Rev. Brownlow told the boys the latest news from Antrim. The new pier was coming along well. The Metho-

dists had built a new church. The lumber hooker that had grounded on Fox Island in the spring finally had been towed into Elk Rapids. When he left, Tommy was smiling, and Herman walked with him to the road again.

From that day on, Jacob taught Tommy a little bit each evening. Herman and Theo tried to learn, too, but gave up quickly each time, yawning and nodding their way to bed each night.

Sooner than he had hoped, Tommy's leg seemed ready for use again. By the middle of July, he was sitting each day swinging his legs over the side of the bed. Only for a little time, during the night, was he forced to lie with his leg splinted. Jacob no longer had to exercise the leg; Tommy could do it himself now.

One day, when dark clouds hung over the bay and hot, angry winds blew swirls of dust from the corn fields, Herman came in at noon to find Tommy on his feet, clinging with both hands to the door frame from the bedroom. Herman looked once and then backed out the cabin door, calling over his shoulder,

"Hurry, Papa! Tommy is out of bed!"

Jacob and Theo came up quickly behind Herman, and pushing him before them, rushed to Tommy.

"Son, son!" cried Jacob, taking one arm as Theo took the other, "you shouldn't have done this!"

"But I'm fine, Father," said Tommy shakily. "It was so hot lying on the bed and I could feel the wind coming in the door, so I thought I'd stand there for a few minutes."

"Well, well, I suppose you must try. But you should have waited for me to help you." Jacob and Theo slowly moved Tommy into the bedroom and helped him raise himself onto the bed.

"But I must walk again, Father," said Tommy.

96

"You will, my son, you will."

"Did it hurt, Tommy?" asked Theo.

"Not much," said Tommy and squared his shoulders. Nonchalantly he picked up the primer that lay by his pillow.

"Then maybe he should try more often, Papa," said Theo.

"Yes, yes, we'll see, we'll see." Jacob left the bedroom and went to the table where Herman, listening hard to the conversation in the bedroom, was spreading applesauce on big pieces of bread.

Theo and Tommy looked at each other after Jacob had left the room.

"I must try, Theo," said Tommy in a low voice. Theo nodded, but did not speak. In a moment, he left the room.

The storm broke then and Herman rushed to close the door. Jacob shivered and quickly laid a fire in the fireplace, lighting it with an awkward, ancient tinderbox, while big drops splashed now and then on the kindling.

Whenever he could, in the next weeks, Tommy crept from his bed and took short, shuffling walks: painfully at first, and then more easily. To the door and back; then, to the table and back; finally, easily around both the rooms of the cabin. One day, finding out from Theo that all three of the others would be in the hay field on the other side of the hill, Tommy ventured into the farmyard. First, he walked to the well. He stood there a moment, a great smile on his face, watching the cow move one slow leg after the other as she cropped the sloping pasture, back of the barn. Then he watched a little group of meadowlarks feeding near the cabin. From across the bay, very faintly, he could hear a frantic boat whistle. The sun was very warm, but the breeze was steady and it soughed in the pines beside the house in a soothing song.

"Tom! Tom!" It was Herman, breathless and frightened, running over the hill and down beside the pasture with giant leaps.

Tommy waited for him beside the well. When Herman reached him, he gasped,

"It's Father, get help!"

Clinging to the well coping with one hand, Tommy gripped Herman's shoulder with the other.

"What is it? Tell me, tell me!"

"I don't know, I don't know," Herman wept, "but he fell down and Theo said he must go home, but he can't walk."

"Run down to Leander's! It's Monday, he'll be home. Quickly!"

Tommy pushed Herman toward the road.

Looking toward the hill again, Tommy saw Theo's sturdy figure silhouetted against the blue summer sky. He lifted his hand and waved to Theo; then standing straight and unaided, he walked slowly toward the house.

9
A Prayer for Papa

Jacob was in bed again.

Theo, Tommy, and Herman stood very still, just outside the bedroom door as Dr. Ingoldsby finished examining their father's back. Leander stood behind them, mumbling, twisting his ancient straw hat, rubbing his stubble of a beard.

Dr. Ingoldsby said a few words to Jacob, but the boys could not hear them.

"Yes, Doctor, I understand," said Jacob.

The doctor came into the other room.

"Boys, your father is very sick. Sicker, I think, than last winter. It is fortunate that I was in Antrim when this happened."

Theo's face went white and two tears rolled down Herman's cheeks.

"What can we do, Doctor?" said Tommy.

"See that he stays in bed and does nothing to aggravate his back." The doctor ran his hand through his hair in a worried gesture. "I wish I could tell you more, I truly do," he went on, "but there is nothing else to do."

"We'll see to it, Doc," put in Leander.

Tommy glared at the old man, who ducked his head and turned away.

"Call on Leander, boys, if you need help," said Dr. Ingoldsby, "He knows a lot about nursing. Mrs. Boyle was sick for many years."

"But I don't know . . ." Tommy started to speak.

"Well, it isn't important now, but remember, he can help you."

"When will he, I mean, will Father be well . . . soon?" asked Herman.

"I don't know, I don't know, I don't know," said the doctor, hurriedly packing his stethoscope, and brushing his hat with his sleeve. "I'll be back in three weeks." He hurried toward the door

"Thank you, Doctor," said Theo.

Leander hurried after the doctor.

"I'll walk ya' to Antrim, Doc!" he called. "'Bye, lads. Come by if ya' need me." He paused and looked at the three before he stepped into the sun.

"'Bye!" shouted Herman, after Leander had gone.

August came, hot and dry. The corn was as tall as it would ever be, but disappointingly scrawny and the ears thin and dry. The potatoes looked better, but until they were harvested, no one could say for certain. The few apple trees, halfway up the hill behind the barn, looked better. The fruit was large and sound and Theo kept some in the bucket down the well because his father liked the crisp crunch and the foamy juice of a barely ripe apple.

100

"He doesn't care for much else, really," Theo told Rev. Brownlow and his wife as they came for a visit one day.

The big man shook his head sadly and Mrs. Brownlow patted Theo's arm without a word.

"But he will like to see you, Reverend, sir."

He led them through the cabin where Tommy was sweeping and Herman washing the dinner dishes. Mrs. Brownlow smiled at both boys.

"Thomas and Herman. How are you, boys? Tommy, how is your leg?"

"Just fine, thank you, ma'm."

"No, it hurts him, I know," said Herman defiantly.

Tommy looked at his brother with surprise.

"Well," he said, "but it gets better all the time."

Herman grunted.

"Good," said Mrs. Brownlow, heartily, "but be sure to get as much rest as you can. Here. I brought some chicken and some biscuits for all of you." She took a checked towel from the top of a basket she held on her arm.

Herman grinned and, putting down the cup he was drying, bent over the basket, breathing deeply.

"Thank you, Mrs. Brownlow," said Theo with a reproving look at his brother.

"Thank you, Mrs. Brownlow," echoed Tommy and Herman together as they put the contents of the basket on the table.

"You are welcome, I'm sure," said Mrs. Brownlow with a laugh.

In the meantime, Rev. Brownlow had stepped to Jacob's bedside and held the sick man's hand for a few minutes.

"We hope you will be getting well soon, Jacob."

101

"I have little hope, Rev. Brownlow," he answered in a low voice.

"That isn't like you, Jacob. You have always been such a hopeful person."

"Ah, but now, now I feel that hope is useless."

Rev. Brownlow stood silent a moment, patting the other man's hand in an absent fashion.

"Jacob, you must then prepare yourself for what is to come. I wish I could help you, but I feel that you would rather do this in your own way."

"I am grateful for your words. You have been a friend, even though I have refused to embrace your faith."

"Oh, Brother Escher, that is the great thing about this land. We can be friends no matter how we pray."

"That is true," said Jacob, with a weak smile, "I have never been sorry I came here." He stopped and turned his eyes to the little window. "Until now, perhaps," he finished softly.

"Why now, Jacob?"

"This." He handed the minister a letter. When Rev. Brownlow had finished reading it, he folded it slowly and handed it back.

"Yes, I see. It is hard to lose a dear sister so many thousands of miles away. Even harder, perhaps, than if you had been there."

Jacob's eyes were filled with tears.

"Why don't you write a letter to your brother?" said Rev. Brownlow.

"Perhaps I shall. It will bring me closer to the old life," Jacob answered, but his voice was listless.

Mrs. Brownlow came in then with the boys, and after they had chatted for several minutes, the minister and his wife left the little family, the cabin standing sharp and clear beneath the ragged, brooding pines.

For the three boys, the days of late summer hurried by, with each day bringing more and more to do. Jacob fretted from his bed as he glimpsed them coming and going. A fox killed some of the chickens and Theo slept for three nights under the stars, waiting for the small thief to return, but he never did. In the evenings, the boys listened carefully while their father told them what must be done the next day. This was harvest time and the time was crowded with special things that must be done.

Tommy saw the slight shake
of the head

Jacob struggled to his feet one day, the boys protesting all the time, and made his way to the cornfield, where he helped pick the corn and then cut and shocked the stalks. They finished only part of the field and by evening Jacob was in bed, his back in agony. Now a fever racked his body, and day after day it stayed high. He was frequently delirious and only their knowledge of his goodness kept the boys from being frightened at his ravings.

One day, at the end of August, he seemed to Theo much weaker than ever before and he sent Herman for Rev. Brownlow. On the way to Antrim, Herman, tears streaming down his face, met Leander. Herman told him of the trouble and the old fisherman started toward the Escher cabin.

When Herman arrived with Rev. Brownlow, Leander was sitting beside the bed, holding Jacob's hand. Theo

103

and Tommy watched quietly from the other side of the bed, Theo holding his father's other hand. Leander was singing very softly to the man on the bed, who now lay very still, a faint smile on his lips.

Rev. Brownlow and Leander looked at each other for a moment and Tommy saw the slight shake of the head that Leander gave the minister. Tommy put his head on his arms and sobs shook his shoulders.

Afternoon turned into evening and evening into night. Theo sent Herman to bed, where the boy cried himself to sleep. Theo and Tommy sat on the floor beside the bed, listening to Rev. Brownlow and Leander singing hymns. Leander's voice was small and high, but Rev. Brownlow's was deep and he sang with a volume that filled the tiny room.

Toward morning Jacob died, quietly, the fever gone, the agony ended, his thoughts winging at last over the blue lakes and mountain villages that he loved.

Rev. Brownlow motioned to Tommy and Theo and Leander and the four knelt beside Jacob's bed and prayed silently for a moment.

10
To Go to School?

Ed Goodspeed made Jacob's coffin. It was a plain pine box, but carefully finished. Rev. Brownlow planned the simple ceremony.

Mrs. Brownlow and Mrs. McDavitt and two ladies from the Methodist church helped the boys prepare for the funeral. Herman sat dazedly by the fire while the women swept and scrubbed the cabin. Tommy and Theo, tears running down their faces, brought in firewood, milked the cow, finished picking the corn and, finally, helped dig a grave beside their long-dead sister on the hill above the farm.

Leander came to the funeral. Supervisor McDavitt, Dr. Belliger, and their wives were there. Two German immigrants from Elk Rapids, who had enjoyed conversations with Jacob in their native tongue, came by boat up Torch Lake and would fish for bass on their way home. 'Dolf Escher, a cousin whom Jacob had helped when 'Dolf was new to America, came all the way from Traverse City on the *Sunnyside*. Aside from Jacob's sons, he was the only member of Jacob's family who saw him buried.

Herman stood trustingly beside the young man as Rev. Brownlow conducted the service. Tommy and Theo eyed 'Dolf thoughtfully and moved closer to him as the small gathering sang a final hymn and Leander and Herr Schmidt lowered the coffin into the grave.

"Boys," said Rev. Brownlow gently, "why don't you, each of you, throw a little dirt onto your father's coffin." He looked at the three stricken faces before him and added, "It helps, lads, believe me it does."

Theo, Tommy, and Herman each bent slowly and took a handful of the thin soil that lay beside the grave. Slowly, each let his handful drop hollowly on the coffin.

And then it was over. Those who had come to the funeral stopped at the cabin and had a cup of Mrs. Brownlow's coffee and a piece of strudel sent by the wife of one of Jacob's German friends. Mrs. McDavitt had brought a ham and a pile of plates. Everyone ate some ham, with a piece of bread and butter from the Methodist ladies.

Herman watched the guests eating. Mrs. Belliger, a small, soft young lady, urged him to eat and brought him a plate of strudel, but his eyes were on 'Dolf now and he did not listen. Theo and Tommy held plates, too, but did not eat. Rev. Brownlow and the German friends talked to them quietly.

"You'll need help to run the farm next year," said Rev. Brownlow. "Perhaps you would like to have me find someone to work it on shares for you."

"No," said Theo firmly and quickly. "It must stay in the family. Father would have wanted it that way."

He continued to look at 'Dolf. Rev. Brownlow followed his gaze.

"I don't think you can expect much help there, son. He hasn't visited your father in over a year, even though he knew of the trouble."

"But we are his family. Now, we four are the only Eschers left in America."

"I vish you luck," said Herr Schmidt with a snort. "On the odder hand, Peter here and I vill be more than delighted to have this young man come mit us to our town where he can go to school there and my good wife could look after his socks and things." The man laughed kindly.

"Thank you, sir, but I must stay here. Father wanted us to stay, all of us."

"It may be a hard winter, Theo, with the poor crop," said Rev. Brownlow warningly.

"We will be all right," said Theo stubbornly.

"If 'Dolf will come next spring to help, or if he will help us pay Mr. Goodspeed, only," said Tommy eagerly, "we will be all right."

"Ho!" said Herr Schmidt, "if that is all," and reached into his pockct.

"No, thank you, sir," said Theo, putting a hand on his arm.

"You see," said Tommy as if explaining again to a very small child, "'Dolf is our cousin and he will want to see that we are all right."

Herr Schmidt looked doubtfully across the room at 'Dolf. The young man stood alone, by the fireplace, a plate of ham, bread and butter and strudel in his hand. His collar was very high and very stiff. His coat was light grey, and his flowing cravat matched it perfectly. Now and then he smoothed his black hair.

107

"A man has his future to think of"

"Vell," continued Herr Schmidt, "please do not vait for catastrophe to call on me." He bowed formally, but continued to stand beside Tommy and Theo.

Before anyone had prepared to leave, Theo, Tommy, and Herman saw that 'Dolf had put down his plate, bowed elegantly to Mrs. McDavitt and Mrs. Brownlow, spoken a few words to Mr. McDavitt and prepared to leave the cabin. The boys all moved toward him.

"Oh, there you are, boys," said 'Dolf as they approached him. "I must be on my way back to Antrim. There's a boat back to Traverse City in the morning. Sorry about Jacob. He was quite a decent sort." He put out his hand to Theo, but Theo only looked at it in horror.

"But we thought . . . I mean, aren't you going to stay a little while?"

"Yes, you're the only relative we have in this country," said Tommy anxiously.

"Well, you know, boys, a man has his future to think of," said 'Dolf, pulling on a pair of yellow kid gloves. "Yes, it's too bad Jacob didn't do better in America." There was almost a question in his voice.

"Oh," said Herman eagerly, "but he did. We had a fire, you see, that's why all the books 'n' things are gone. We didn't have to *sell* them," he finished, recalling tales of other hard-pressed settlers who lived for many months on money from selling family heirlooms.

"Oh?"

"Yes, Cousin, we have eighty acres and in a couple of years it will all be under cultivation. Father says . . . ," and Tommy stopped, remembering.

'Dolf had lost interest at this point and turned again to the door.

"Good-bye, lads, and if you're ever in Traverse City, please drop in to see me. You have my address, I believe?"

"Yes, Cou . . . , yes, we have it," said Theo.

"Good-bye," said Tommy and Herman quietly.

Rev. Brownlow put an arm across Theo's shoulders and said, "Probably he intends to come back in the spring and help with the planting?"

Theo looked without expression at the kindly man.

"Thank you, sir, but I expect we'll do the planting ourselves."

"Not alone, surely. There are many of us who will be delighted to help, you know. We loved your father and admire you boys' courage."

Theo reddened.

"Thank you, Reverend," said Tommy, "but Father never asked for help and we won't either."

Rev. Brownlow said nothing for several minutes.

The women were washing the cups and plates now and wrapping the leftover food carefully and storing it in the corner cupboard. It was just a little after noon and several of the men had stepped outside to look at the haze that hung over the bay.

"Well, are you boys all going to school this winter?" asked the minister.

The boys looked at him in amazement.

"It'll be starting next week," Rev. Brownlow went on.

109

"We know, sir, and we did think maybe we would send Herman. . . ." Theo's voice trailed off.

"Oh, as to that, you should all go. There's hardly a man of any importance at all nowadays who can't write and figure."

"Yes, but. . . ."

"The crops are all in, surely?"

"Yeeeess, but. . . ."

"Well, then?"

Tommy looked at his older brother anxiously.

"Well, we'll see," said Theo.

"I hope it's yes," said Rev. Brownlow with a smile.

In a few minutes the visitors began to leave, each with a kind word and a generous offer for the boys. Shortly, they were alone in the cabin, which was as neat and clean as the women could make it. Theo looked around.

"Could we, Theo, could we?"

"What, Tommy?" he asked absently.

"Go to school. You know."

"Oh, that. I s'pose so."

Tommy looked gratified.

There was a soft knock on the front door. Herman ran to open it. Mr. Goodspeed stood in the doorway.

"Say, boys, about your Pa's coffin. . . ."

"Yes, sir?" said Herman.

"Well, I hope it pleased ya'."

"Oh, yes, it was very nice, Mr. Goodspeed," said Tommy.

"Good, good." He paused. "Don't 'spect he left you any too well off, now, did he?"

Theo, who was expecting another offer of help, said, "Oh, we're fine, sir, thank you."

"Good, good. 'Cause I put a lot of work on that box.

Nice one. Fifteen-dollar box, if I ever made one." He stood in the doorway without moving.

Theo realized now why he had come.

"Oh, we'll pay you. Mr. Goodspeed, never fear."

"Good, good. Could give it to you. Charity, like, but didn't suppose you boys'd want that. No, sir."

"That's right, we don't. You'll get your money as soon as we can sell the potatoes and . . . and. . . ." Tommy's voice trailed off.

". . . and get some work," said Theo.

". . . after school," finished Herman.

"Good, good. No hurry, 'course. Sorry about your paw, boys. Good-bye to you." Mr. Goodspeed turned hurriedly and walked away across the farmyard.

"About your Pa's coffin . . .

"Why did you say that about the potatoes?" asked Theo.

"Well, it's all we got. What else can we sell? We sold the corn and all the chickens to pay Dr. Ingoldsby all we could and nobody needs milk and . . . well, that's all that's left."

"Yes, yes, that's right." Theo sounded worried.

"What's the matter, Theo?" said Herman, clutching at his older brother's sleeve.

"Nothing, nothing. I guess we got enough potatoes and turnips to sell some, but it won't bring fifteen dollars.

"Course not," said Tommy, confidently, "but Mrs. McDavitt told Mrs. Belliger that she had nobody to cut wood for her this fall. I heard her, and I thought we could ask for the job."

"Sure," said Theo, "there's still time 'til first frost and we could work on it all day on Saturday and maybe some after school. . . ." He stopped short and reddened.

"Then we really can go," said Tommy with finality.

"Oh, I s'pose we should."

Herman burst into tears. "Papa, Papa!" he cried over and over again.

Theo looked at him with dismay.

"Why, Herman, why are you crying like that?"

"Because he didn't get to hear me read," sobbed the youngest boy.

Theo and Tommy sat for a few minutes, tears silently welling in their own eyes.

"I don't know, Theo," said Tommy in a choked voice, "maybe we can't. . . ."

"What else can we do? We'll do it, is all." Theo straightened his shoulders and put his chin out firmly.

". . . and next spring," Tommy went on, "Papa

wanted to clear some more land to plant beans. Remember?"

". . . but without any help at all, and Cousin 'Dolf. . . ."

"Maybe he will come back," interrupted Herman, who had stopped sobbing. He wiped his eyes with his sleeve.

"What'll we do? We'll have to ask him, anyway," said Theo. "We've got to make out some way."

"I hope so," said Tommy.

"We will," said Herman, unsmiling.

11
Forest Fire!

Outside the small schoolhouse, in the dusty yard, the wind blew gusts now and then, rattling the dry and dusty leaves in the maples along the fence. It was the middle of October and school had been in session for almost a week now.

"Rrriiinnnnngggg!"

Theo, standing with fourteen other children waiting to be dismissed, wondered why the bell had to be so loud and why Mr. Weaver had it ring at all. After all, they were all right there, couldn't he just say "Dismissed?"

He asked Danny Sloane a few minutes later as they walked across the school grounds, books swinging at their sides.

"Well, it's such a loud bell that Mrs. Weaver can hear it, 'way down to his house." Danny gestured toward the end of the street that ran at right angles to the road on which the schoolhouse stood. "Anyway, when she hears it, she puts on the coffeepot and cuts the pie. He's more'n a mite hungry when he gets home."

Theo laughed and said, "Who isn't?" He waved good-bye to Danny at the schoolyard gate and caught up with his brothers who were walking slowly toward the Flat Road.

"Do you smell it?" called Herman as Theo came nearer.

"Yes. There's fire someplace."

"Most likely a long way off," said Tommy. He stood a little farther up the hill than his brothers. He was above the roofs and the trees of the village now and could see out to the bay.

"Why?" asked Theo.

"Well, it seem to be coming up from Traverse City." His two brothers joined him and looked over the water, straining their eyes to see through the gray haze that seemed to thicken as they watched.

"Well, it's not around here or we'd have heard the fire bells," said Tommy.

". . . and Mr. Weaver would have gone, too," finished Herman.

"Yes. Well, you go on home, Herman, and don't forget to milk the cow. Tommy and I are going back to McDavitt's and finish cutting their wood."

"How much money do we have?" asked Herman worriedly.

"Oh, with the potato money and what we got last week and what Mrs. McDavitt'll give us tomorrow, I guess we'll only have to work a couple more weeks." Theo spoke nonchalantly and Herman looked at him gratefully.

Theo smiled at Herman and rubbed his brother's head.

"I'm the man. Let me do the worrying. G' bye."

The boys separated at the Flat Road, Herman going toward home and Theo and Tommy heading north toward Mr. McDavitt's small chicken farm.

When they reached the farm and reported to Mrs. McDavitt, she came out on her back stoop. She was a tall woman, solidly built, with a placid air about her.

"There's the woodpile, boys. Think you can finish today?"

"Yes'm, I guess so," said Theo.

"Good. I'll pay you today, if you do, so's you won't have to tramp all the way back here tomorrow. My, there's a lot of smoke in the air, isn't there?" She waved her apron lazily in front of her a few times.

"Yes'm, there sure is," said Tommy interestedly.

"Probably from Chicago . . . heard it's burning down."

"What?!" Tommy and Theo spoke together.

"Yes. So I hear from Ben McIntyre, who come up from Traverse City this mornin' to start settin' up the winter camps."

Theo and Tommy looked at each other in wonder. They had been through Chicago as very small boys, on the way here from their first American home in Missouri. They could hardly believe that such a vastness of solidity could be consumed by smoke in the very same way as their first flimsy cabin had been. If it were so — and Ben McIntyre was a straightforward, truthful man, they knew — then any sort of fire was possible. They had seen smaller forest fires in the past; they had heard tales, folk legends passed down by the Indians, of fire sweeping the land for miles on miles in the generations long gone. But this fall fire seemed to them much closer than it ever had before. Some days, as they came down the road to town on their way to school, they could barely make out the end of the Antrim pier, the pall of smoke from distant fires so filled the air. They heard, too, of ships groping their way through the smoke. Sometimes there were disasters and ships would collide far out on the lake, so heavy hung the smoke.

Some days, of course, the breeze was strong and the only evidence of far-off fires was the curious color of the sun and the greyish cloud that swept thinly across the upper sky.

They never became used to the smell. Each day the smell of smoke rang alarms in their minds and Herman dreamed almost always of their first house burning to the ground. The sound of his father's sobs, recalled from the dreams, haunted his days. Theo and Tommy had more practical fears.

Mrs. McDavitt waved her apron once more and went back into the kitchen. Theo and Tommy moved slowly to the woodpile and, putting their books and jackets carefully in the crotch of a nearby apple tree, picked up their axes and went to work.

"Let's go as fast as we can," said Theo.

"Yes," Tommy replied shortly, swinging his axe as quickly and accurately as he could.

The boys worked without speaking. The pile of split logs grew steadily and before the sun touched the tops of the tree between McDavitt's and the lake-shore cliff, the·boys had finished the job. They hastily cleaned up the corner of the yard where they had been working and, picking up their things, ran to the McDavitt's back door. Mrs. McDavitt came promptly to the door and gave the boys a handful of coins.

"You're welcome to stay for dinner, if you'd care to." She smiled down at them.

"Thank you, Ma'am. That's nice of you, but Herman is home and we'd best be getting back."

"Of course. Well, you're good workers and you can cut wood for me next year, if you'd care to."

Tommy smiled at her and Theo said, "Thank you, Mrs. McDavitt."

When she had gone back into the house, the boys ran from the yard. Down the Flat Road they streaked, apprehension driving them on. They rested briefly near Leander's and saw that there was no more smoke than usual over their own farm some distance ahead.

After that, they walked. Worry still lined Theo's forehead, but Tommy gave a skip of relief. He crossed the road to a stately, well-shaped beech tree that had been spared for some unknown reason when the land had been logged. The leaves were faintly tinged with yellow and the small, prickly nut cases had begun to drop. Tommy flung his coat down and scooped handfuls of nuts, well mixed with leaves, twigs, and sandy soil, into his coat and then flung it like a sack over his shoulder.

"Are they ripe yet?" asked Theo doubtfully.

"Mostly. We'll roast 'em and they'll be as good as bread tonight. Before we go to bed."

"No fires. Not after supper. You know that," said Theo sternly.

"Oh, I forgot." Tommy seemed momentarily saddened, but he cheered up quickly and said, "I'll put 'em in the loft and that'll give 'em a chance to ripen. Then, soon's it rains, we'll have a fire and roast 'em."

Theo nodded without speaking and the boys continued down the road and across their farmyard and into the front door.

"Chicago's burning down!" said Tommy briskly as he entered the door.

"Oh? What's a chicago?" asked Herman, who squatted beside the fireplace, stirring a kettle of stew.

Theo's brow cleared and he laughed.

"It's a place, ninny," said Tommy crossly.

Herman thought for a moment or two.

"Oh, yes," he said finally, "I guess I remember Papa telling about it."

Theo smiled kindly at his brother and helped put plates and forks on the table.

"Well, we've got almost enough to pay Mr. Goodspeed. Another week and we will."

"Where'll we go next week?" asked Tommy.

"Leander said he'd give us something if we'll help with his winter lines."

"Ugh," said Tommy, who hated the tedious untangling and tying.

"Well, it's work."

"Ummmm," answered Tommy.

That evening, after the dishes had been washed, the boys walked down to the creek that ran along one boundary of their land. Their father had built the barn only a little distance from the creek so that there would be water close by for the animals, and to fight a fire, if it should be necessary. The first story of the barn was native stone, but the loft and the corncrib beside the barn were built of wood and filled with the dry hay and fodder the boys had harvested that summer with the final help of their father.

Now they looked across the stream. Its bed was about twelve feet wide, but it was shrunken by the dry fall to about half the width of its bed. Theo wondered if it wouldn't have been better to have built a little farther from the stream, and also a little farther from the tinder-box that lay beyond. The acreage there was still owned by the railroad. It was for sale, but so far no one had seemed interested. Covered as it was with a stand of second growth, and the forest floor thick with fallen snags and deadheads, it was like a giant fireplace.

The sun had disappeared an hour before and only its feverish reflection clung to the clouds above the bay. The little stream caught the hue and flung it back at the boys like a dream of fire. Theo could not see into the woods beyond the stream, but he knew what lay there and he shivered.

The three boys spread their pallets on the ground floor of the cabin these nights. The loft was very hot, for one thing, and for another, Leander Boyle had told them they should.

He had come one day to bring the boys a string of fish and to show them how to smoke them for the winter.

"It's like a box o' straw, boys, this whole side o' the state. One spark and, whoosh, up she goes. Don't get caught up there sleepin'." He had said no more, but Theo had understood and a few nights after their first day at school, he had dragged their pallets downstairs. Herman had looked at him in amazement, but Tommy understood. Each day they stacked them in their father's bedroom.

"We'll build very small fires to cook on," Theo had said, moving the kindling box to the other side of the room, away from the fireplace, "and we'll put the fire out, always, after we've eaten."

"But we'll freeze in the morning," Herman had protested.

121

"For heaven's sake, it's so warm we can hardly stand it. What are you talking about?"

"Well, it won't be this winter."

"This winter," Theo had said with exaggerated patience, "we'll be upstairs again and the danger of fire will be passed."

"Oh." Herman had thought for a few minutes. "I see. Leander meant the railroad property might catch fire and spread to our house." Herman had shivered and helped Theo put out the small breakfast fire.

Often at night Tommy would half waken to find Theo gone from his pallet. Tommy knew that he was standing outside the door, his head raised, sniffing the eternal smoke. Usually Tommy dozed off again without getting up, but tonight he joined his brother at the door. They stood silently for a few minutes.

"You look like a rabbit," said Tommy scornfully.

Theo did not answer, but continued turning his head, breathing in the heavy air.

"Theo, nothing's going to happen here," Tommy began. "All the fires are far away."

"Not all."

"What do you mean?"

"I don't know exactly, but I'm sure there's something closer."

The wind was strong tonight, but even so it did not clear the air of smoke. Tommy moved uneasily.

"Let's go back to sleep, Theo." Both boys turned into the house and without another word climbed into their beds. Herman slept on. Tommy turned over and the next thing he knew, someone was shouting his name.

"Tommy! Tommy!" He woke suddenly and sat up instantly.

122

"Get your pants on! There's fire across the creek!"
Theo shouted.

Herman and Tommy scrambled into their clothes as
fast as they could and followed Theo out the door into
the farmyard. The grayness of the sky meant morning
had almost come, but the darkness had not lifted from
the yard. The twilight was made of smoke, pushed in a
steady cloud by the strong west winds.

Tommy and Herman saw a figure running ahead of
Theo. It was Leander. In each hand he carried a
mattock and behind him Theo carried an axe and a
shovel. Tommy looked around the door yard and grabbed a saw, the only tool he could see. Herman, however,
darted around the far end of the cabin and returned
with a short-handled shovel.

The fire had started near the Flat Road, a hundred
yards or so south of where the road crossed the creek that
bounded the Escher farm on the south and east. Pushed
by the strong south wind, it had moved straight north
along the road, fanning out all the time until it had
reached the creek. Then, not able to cross the creek,
which became wider the closer to the shore it ran,
the fire had moved swiftly along its banks. When
Leander, on his way to Torch Lake, discovered it just
before dawn, the fire had moved up the creek bank so
that it was opposite the cabin. It reached greedily across
the stream, but there was nothing to help it across the
water. The wind shifted slightly now and then, coming
from the southwest, so that its progress up the little water-
course was now sometimes swift, sometimes slow.

When the boys came out of their house, they could
not see the fire at all, only the dense black smoke. As
they raced across the yard behind Leander, they could
hear it more clearly but still could not see it. When

they reached their side of the stream, they turned north-east to run beside the water, still following Leander.

"Why . . . why . . . are we going away from it?!" shouted Tommy.

No one answered him, but in a few minutes he saw why. They came to a place where the creek narrowed and ran between higher banks, through a small hill. If the fire reached this far, it would be able to jump to the Escher side of the creek.

"Cut away everything!"

"Boys! Listen!" said Leander. "I'm goin' to the other side and cut a fire lane, if I can, just enough to keep it from headin' any farther north. There's not much more for it to feed on anyway, north o' here, and if we can keep 'er here, the wind at her back'll have her out in no time."

"What should we do?" asked Theo.

"Do! Why, you stay here and cut away everything you can, right down to bare earth, and keep 'er from jumpin' the creek." He said no more, but when they looked behind them, the boys understood. If the fire jumped here, it would spread instantly to their barn. It was a nightmare Theo had dreamed often enough.

They could hear the crackling of the flames now, and with the wind blowing the smoke across the creek a little way downstream, they were enough beyond the main part of the smoke so that now and again they could see the orange flames.

"Lucky in a way that's all been logged off. Nothin' tall there to crown. Keeps it close to the ground," Leander said cheerfully. He jumped down into the creek bed and, using his hat as a basin, poured water over himself.

The boys began clearing the ground on their side of the creek, starting at the base of the little hill. There were no trees on the very top of the little hill, on either side of the creek, and the boys could hear Leander's mattock ringing now and then as he moved away from them, scraping, grubbing and hacking at everything that stood along his way. The path was not wide, not as wide as a safe fire lane should be, perhaps, but Leander made very certain no dry twigs crossed it like a bridge for the fire.

The fire was not far away, now. It had almost reached the foot of the hill on the other side of the creek.

Theo scraped with Leander's other mattock. Tommy

and Herman scraped with their shovels. The heat from
the fire reached them in all its force now. They worked
frantically, knowing when the full force of the smoke
crossed the stream in their direction they would not be
able to stay for long where they were. The clean area
beside the stream grew steadily. Soon, though, they
could hardly see the ground at their feet and their eyes
wept constantly. They coughed and choked.

"Run, boys, downstream!" shouted Theo.

Herman and Tommy stumbled quickly after their
brother down the hill. The smoke was much thinner
here, now. The fire was dying at the road end of the
stream and slowly becoming less fierce as it consumed
all the fuel along the way up the stream.

The boys flung themselves to the ground a little way
from the foot of the hill.

"Can't . . . we . . . go farther . . . away?" gasped
Herman.

"No," said Theo, panting. "We've got to watch for
sparks."

"But we can't see them from here," said Tommy.

"I know, I know. We'll have to back up every few
minutes." So saying, he picked up the mattock and ran
up the hill again, his sleeve over his face. Herman and
Tommy saw him disappear into the smoke. A few
minutes later he returned. He said nothing but lay
panting beside his brothers.

"I'm next," said Tommy, and he, too, went up the
hill.

Herman took a turn after that, and the brothers
alternated that way for a time that seemed like forever.
Soon, though, the smoke was less and the two brothers
lying at the bottom of the hill could see the third quite
clearly almost to the top. And soon they were able to go

up together and stay, walking slowly about, eyes always watchful for anything coming through the thinning smoke from the other side.

Now they could see the other side. Straight away from the top of the hill stretched Leander's fire lane.

"I think I'll go over and help," said Theo, and without waiting he ran and jumped across the narrow gap.

"Me, too," said Tommy, and followed. Herman was about to do so, also, when he looked back and saw a spark land behind him, almost crossing the bare earth they had cleared. He beat at it with his shovel and stayed on his side of the stream.

Theo and Tommy patrolled the upper side of the fire lane for some time. Now and then, even though the upper side held only some weeds and a few blackberry bushes, the fire would cross and start a fierce little blaze.

They saw no sign of Leander.

"Well, I guess he's all right," said Theo.

"How can we be sure?" asked Tommy.

"Well, we can't but I've been down as far as the fire lane goes, all the way to Hackett's back fence and the fire's out, far's I can see, but I didn't see Leander."

"I suppose he went on down fishing," Tommy spoke uneasily.

Back home, Herman finally had decided to go in and get some breakfast. He fixed cornbread and syrup and then carried pieces of it on a plate to the top of the hill.

"Theo, Tommy!" he called, and waited. "Theo, Tommy!" again. "Come and have breakfast!" He waited only a moment and then heard from the other side, the thump and scrape of the mattock and the shovel as the boys used them climbing the hill.

They jumped across the stream and, flinging them-

selves and their tools wearily on the ground, reached
for a piece of the bread Herman offered.

"Where's Leander?" asked Herman.

"Here I am, boy. Did you say breakfast?"

All three boys turned to see the tall figure climbing
the hill from the north side.

Without a word, Herman passed the tin plate of bread
and Leander helped himself to a slice.

"Well, that wasn't much of a fire," said Leander at
last.

Theo and Tommy looked crestfallen.

"Might 'a been, tho," went on Leander, "coulda
took the whole dang farm, it coulda." He smacked his
lips and reached for another piece of bread.

Theo and Tommy brightened.

"Yup, you kin tell 'em at the school . . . ," — the three
boys looked startled and scrambled hastily to their feet —
". . . when ya' go this afternoon, that you've fought an
A-1 forest fire."

"This afternoon?"

"Well, what time you think it is?" Leander looked
at the sun. "I figure it's about eleven."

"That late!" exclaimed Tommy.

"Yup. When I passed the barn a bit ago, seemed like
there was a mighty unhappy cow in there." Leander
wiped his hands on the seat of his pants. He picked
up his two mattocks and started toward the road. "Bye,
boys," he said casually.

"Good-bye, Leander," said the boys together, and
Tommy ran after him a few steps.

". . . and, and . . . thank you, thank you!" he called
after the tall figure. Leander waved without looking
at them.

12
Off to North Camp

After the fires and the smoke, the north winds began to howl across the bay. Straight across Wisconsin from Canada they came. The lakes were still open at the end of November, but each week fewer and fewer ships came to the pier at Antrim. Many shipmasters were fearful of being frozen in at a strange harbor, hundreds of miles from home, during the long, bitter winter. For some, though, the bounty for racing the last of the cargo ahead of the ice was worth the risk.

Every day the lake was quieter. Soon only the wind would be heard. The rough and dangerous ice shelf, already tumbled with gigantic shards of ice, was built out far enough so that Theo, looking across the bay, could not really tell where the ice ended and open water began.

"I bet he'll be the last," he said one day, peering

at the tiny black puff on the horizon that was a ship on its way out of the Antrim harbor.

"Yes, and there's not much use our being here, either. Come on." Tommy pulled at Theo's arm and they turned to follow Herman up through the trees toward home.

"Let's not come home this way any more," said Herman when the others had joined him.

"Why not?"

"Gettin' too cold," said Herman and huddled miserably inside the thin jacket and scarf he wore.

"I s'pose so. Besides, it'll start to snow soon."

"Yeh, should have by now," said Tommy.

"Well, let's count our blessings."

The boys trudged up the hill and across the Flat Road. Tommy limped in the icy wind and swung two books tied with a string. Theo carried his books and Herman clutched a slate under his arm.

As they crossed the farmyard, Tommy went toward the cow-shed while the other two went into the cabin. The air was very clear and no smoke rose from the cabin chimney. Before he went through the door, Theo grabbed an armload of wood from a pile under the eaves.

Inside, Herman had put down his slate and was scrabbling through the cupboard.

"No flour, no bacon, no sugar," he stated.

"Well, we' don't need 'em anyhow," said Theo cheerfully. "We have some corn meal. . . ."

"Not much. . . ."

". . . and butter and maple syrup."

"*And* milk."

"And milk! So, cut down some leeks and we'll have soup!"

He spoke in a jolly tone and busily went about making a fire in the black grayness of the fireplace.

Herman sighed and went out the door with a small kettle. When he returned with the milk a few minutes later, Theo had a small but hearty blaze going. Herman clambered to the table top and reached up to cut down a bunch of wild leeks that had been hanging from the ceiling beams to dry. They fell from his hands with a papery rattle to the table top.

Several minutes later Tommy came in just as Herman was hanging the kettle from the hook in the fireplace. The air was sharp with the strong onion smell of the leeks.

"Oh, not leek soup again!"

"I put a few potatoes in tonight," said Herman.

"Ah, well . . ." and Tommy's voice trailed off as he warmed his hand momentarily in front of the fire.

When the meal was ready at last, the boys sat down. After a few dismal looks at their bowls, Herman took up his spoon and began to eat his soup noisily. Theo and Tommy followed his example. Big mugs of milk went with the meal and small, crusty johnnycakes with a spoonful of syrup for each.

"We gotta get some more flour," said Theo.

"How?" asked Tommy between bits of johnnycake.

"Well . . . we could help over at the north camp. They always want workers during the winter, to. . . ."

"We're going to school all day, remember?" said Tommy politely.

"Besides, they'd just say I was too small for lumbering," put in Herman.

"Not you, stupid, just Tommy and me."

Herman angrily ate the last potato that lay in his bowl.

Theo and Tommy said no more, but scraped and piled

131

their dishes. Tommy went for a bucket of water and in silence the three boys washed their dishes. Afterward Theo swept the floor while Tommy went out to make sure the cow had enough fodder for the night. Herman went with him as far as the big woodpile near the barn and brought back a huge armload of wood.

Tommy came up as he almost reached the door.

"We . . . really . . . should . . . cut . . . some . . . more," grumbled Herman as he staggered into the cabin with his load.

"Yes, yes, I know. Tomorrow," muttered Tommy.

That evening Theo told Herman to go to bed early. As he climbed the ladder, the younger boy shouted,

"You're going to talk about me! It isn't fair!" When he reached the loft, he lay on the floor, his angry face peering down at his brothers.

"Herman . . . ," said Theo quietly. Herman disappeared from sight and in a few seconds his brothers could hear him settling into his pallet.

Theo and Tommy sat by the fire silently for some time. At last Tommy spoke.

"What should we do?"

"Well, how much food do we have? Right now."

"There's the cow, of course, and we've got enough for her to eat 'til spring, I'm sure," replied Tommy.

"But food for us, for Herman. What about that?" asked Theo.

"The potatoes are about gone . . . wish we hadn't sold so many when Papa died. . . ."

"We'd have a debt, if we didn't, is all," interrupted Theo.

"Ummm," said Tommy, and went on, "So's the corn meal about gone. You know we didn't get much syrup last spring. Not for all the work we put in."

Theo nodded his head at the memory.

"Well, we can't live on leek soup all winter," said Tommy.

"No, not if it doesn't have potatoes we can't."

"Couldn't we ask Rev. Brownlow to lend us some money until next year, and we get the crops in?"

"No," said Theo firmly. "He'd only do it out of kindness, 'cause how could he know whether we could ever pay him back."

Tommy looked at Theo with surprise. Theo seemed to make a decision and, standing suddenly, he faced his brother, his jaw firm.

"Tommy, I'm the man now. I have to be. I decided today, I'm responsible for you and Herman." His voice faltered, but Tommy continued to look at him steadily and went on. "There comes a time when a man has to choose between bread and school."

"Then . . . we have to quit?"

"There's no other way. I . . . I told Mr. Weaver yesterday after school. He knows tomorrow will be our last day. He understands." Theo waited for Tommy's anger.

But Tommy only nodded his head slowly.

"Will they take us at north camp, do you think?"

"We can try." Theo began to bank the fire.

Tommy went for a bucket of water and put it beside the hearth. The boys had found that if they washed their faces and hands well each morning, their teacher was much more pleasant to them that day. It seemed a waste of time to Herman, but if the water was even slightly warm, he would wash himself with only a little bit of grumbling.

It was very dark and cold as the three boys tramped the two miles to the Antrim schoolhouse the next morning. A few flakes of snow were in the air and the hard earth of the road rang underfoot.

Wrapped in a piece of cloth in each boy's pocket was a large slab of cheese. Theo had told Tommy but not Herman that this was the last of the cheese their father had made the past summer, before he became bedridden for the last time. Tommy had asked if they could make cheese, his spirits brightening at the prospect, but Theo did not know how and he didn't think that many people around Antrim made their own cheese.

The day went quickly for Tommy and Theo, each knowing this was their last day of school, perhaps forever.

Finally, the bell rang and Theo and Tommy slowly closed their books and walked out, leaving their slates and books on Mr. Weaver's desk.

The three boys started up the road toward home. When they had almost reached the Flat Road, they met Rev. Brownlow walking quickly down toward the village.

"Hello, boys. I'm glad to see you. How is school?"

"Just fine, sir," said Theo.

"Good, good. Theo, might I speak to you a moment? You run on, boys. I shan't keep him long." Rev. Brownlow waved to Tommy and Herman who started up the road again.

"Yes, sir?" asked Theo politely.

"Theo, are you certain you're getting along all right? Mr. Weaver tells me you and Tommy are leaving school."

Theo hesitated a long time before answering. He

glanced now and then at the patient face above him, and a frown creased his brow under the shock of black hair.

"Well . . . ," he said at last, "we have got to go to work. It'll be winter soon . . . and, well, we haven't much food left, so we need to earn money."

"What had you thought you'd do?" asked the minister.

"We're going to North Camp on Monday and see if they'll have us."

Rev. Brownlow looked at him for several seconds, concern showing in his eyes.

"I wish you good fortune," he said quietly, "and may the good Lord bless your venture."

"Thank you, sir."

"Keep yourselves pure in heart, Theo. Remember, a lumber camp can be a mighty rough place."

Rev. Brownlow paused, and then, instead of continuing down the road, he spoke again. "In fact," he said with a small laugh and a wave of his hand, "Mrs. Brownlow and I were wondering if perhaps it mightn't be easier for everyone if Herman boarded with us here in town during the school year. In a little while, when the snows come, it'll be hard for him to get down here." He stopped.

Theo was silent and the minister went on. "Some nights, in fact," he continued, "you and Theo might not be able to get home from North Camp. You might have to stay there, and Herman would be left alone." He stopped again and looked steadily at Theo's unsmiling face. "Well, think it over, won't you? I'll ask you again in a day or two. Good-bye."

Theo stood in the roadway and watched Rev. Brownlow walk down toward the village. When he had gone twenty feet or so, Theo called after him,

"But, sir, we can't pay you anything for his board."

Huddled against the cold

"Oh, no. That's nothing. There'll be plenty of work for a young lad to pay his way. Don't fret about that. I'll talk to you tomorrow," the man called back, and went on.

"Good-bye, sir. And . . . and . . . thank you!"

By the time he caught up with his brothers, they were well along the Flat Road.

"What did he want?" asked Herman.

"Oh, nothing."

Tommy looked at him curiously, but said nothing. Herman also was quiet. They walked quickly, huddled against the cold, feeling the sting of snow against their faces. By the time they reached the track that led into their own farmyard, the snow had thickened in the air and the day had turned very dark.

"Better give her extra feed tonight. And extra straw!" called Theo as Tommy ran toward the barn.

All through their meager supper, the boys were silent. Herman and Tommy knew that the sadness in Theo's face was not just because the potatoes were nearly gone and flour was gone and there had been no money to buy eggs for weeks. Something else was giving his face the look they had seen on their father's face when he had been forced to stop working that last summer and go to bed again. Finally, as Herman was getting ready to go up to the loft to bed, Theo told them his problem.

"Rev. Brownlow did want something special this afternoon," he said.

Herman exclaimed in surprise, but Tommy said, "Ha! I thought so."

"Yes. He suggested something." Theo stopped and poked rapidly at the fire.

"Well?" asked Tommy.

"He says . . . he thinks . . . well, he thinks maybe Herman ought to stay with them this winter." He paused and looked apprehensively at his brothers. They looked back at him steadily and he went on, "He says it'll be heavy snow soon and hard for him to get down alone and maybe we couldn't get home some nights and, well . . . we've got to do something, I guess."

"I don't want to," said Herman quietly.

"I know," answered Theo.

". . . but I suppose I've got to," Herman finished. He put his elbow on his knee and rested his face in his hands. A tear dripped slowly through his fingers.

"Why? Why should he?" said Tommy loudly and angrily.

"You know, Tommy," said Theo, "it's really the only way. I've thought and thought."

"But we can't pay anything for his board," protested Tommy.

"We wouldn't have to. Herman can do chores, he said. Probably not too hard," said Theo.

The boys were quiet for some time after this, Herman still weeping a little. Gradually Tommy's face lost its anger and assumed a look of resignation. Theo noticed and finally asked,

"Well, what do you think?"

"I guess . . . I guess it'll have to be all right. When should he go?"

"As soon as possible. Rev. Brownlow said he'd talk to me tomorrow." And turning to Herman, "So you'd better take your things with you to school in the morn-

"Take your things with you"

His pitiful collection of worldly goods

ing." Theo spoke firmly and matter-of-factly, but his voice quivered at the end. Herman sobbed openly now, but got up and walked around the room, collecting a scarf here, the pieces of quilt he used around his legs, his other shirt which hung by the fireplace to dry after Tommy had washed it the day before. When he had gathered everything of his own, he started up the ladder to the loft. Tommy and Theo, who stayed downstairs for a moment, could hear him scrambling around overhead, and they knew he was gathering the rest of his pitiful collection of worldly goods.

"We'll take him to school, then go talk to Rev. Brownlow, and then start for North Camp," said Theo in a businesslike voice.

Tommy nodded without a word and the two boys started up the ladder.

13
Herman's Crazy Bear

Herman had a new pair of black serge trousers, heavy and warm and scratchy, and a pair of real mittens, red and warm and soft. On Saturday afternoons and Sundays, when the snow was not too deep, the boys met in Antrim at the Brownlow's house. Sometimes they sat awkwardly in the kitchen, while Mrs. Brownlow fed them gingerbread and sometimes they walked up to the farmhouse and back. This walk, however, made Herman sad, so the boys did it less and less often as the weeks wore on. Tommy was surpised to find that although his own hands were raw and veined with chilblains, he was happy to see that Herman's were warm. Theo took an equally surprised satisfaction in the sight of Herman's bed with real blankets and the teacher's remark, as he had passed him one day, that Herman was becoming a good scholar.

Work in the lumber camp was cruelly hard in the winter. The boys were not big enough to help with the actual felling of the trees, so they found themselves struggling to help attach logs to teams of bullocks, hindered by hip-deep snow. On some nights Tommy's leg ached so that it throbbed until almost dawn.

Sometimes they helped spread more straw on the single-track logging roads that wandered through the forest. The teams of horses and bullocks used these tracks, beaten down and the snow compacted with straw, for pulling the day's cut to small yards dotted convenient-

ly through the woods. When spring came, these logging roads would stand for weeks above the snowless forest floor, so hard and trampled had they become.

Sometimes the boys stayed at the camp and chopped firewood for the cook, or helped the blacksmith. Those were the days they liked best. Even though they scorched their fingers or felt their heads might come off with the ring and clang of the smith's hammer, working at the smithy meant a hot meal at noon and a few more hours indoors, out of the numbing cold. They were given their wages late on Saturday afternoon. The precious few coins went for flour, salt, meat, and sometimes eggs. One time they saved enough to buy Theo a pair of shoes.

The boys were not tall, but their shoulders were broader than those of most boys their age. Still, the huge men with whom they worked made them seem even smaller. Many of the men who worked as loggers during the winter were neighbors and farmers like themselves. Farming was not prosperous around Antrim, although several farmers were now putting all their time and money into fruit trees and doing quite well. The others — those who had to work at North Camp — clung to the same kind of farming their fathers had done in southern Michigan, Ohio, and New England. Every year more families came seeking homestead land and the land the lumber companies and the railroads no longer wanted, but the crops they knew best did poorly here.

Sometimes Theo thought they would cut down every tree in Antrim County. The beech and maple were about gone, down the lake to Chicago; the hemlock, prized so highly by the earlier settlers for its bark, was being cut for pulp, for boxes, for building the villages, towns, and cities that were springing up so quickly east of the Appalachians. Sometimes Theo wanted to cry out against this last particularly. To see the tall, shaggy sentinels that had once darkened all the shore falling to the gleaming axe was almost more than he could bear.

The acres west of their farm, where the boys had helped fight the fire the fall before, had been bought by a Massachusetts family. Leander Boyle snorted when he heard the news at North Camp one February day. He dumped the basket of fish he had caught that morning on the cook's huge wooden table.

"Shoulda left the railroad keep it!"

"How come, Leander?" asked Tommy, who had picked the nearest fish and started to clean it, a regular Friday job for him now.

"No good now, not much good before, after the loggers

were through. No good at all now, after the fire. All the richness burned out. Won't grow nothin', you'll see."

"Less talk, old man!" shouted the cook, who was from Canada and insisted that there be no talk in his kitchen while the cooking was going on.

Leander snuffled a few times and, grumbling quietly, left the kitchen with his basket. Tommy went on scraping the fish.

A few minutes later Theo stumbled into the kitchen with a huge armload of wood. He put it down beside the stove as quietly as possible. He stood for a few minutes, first on one foot, then on the other. He cleared his throat and the cook looked at him fiercely.

"Well, small boy?" He looked Theo up and down. "Large boy?"

"My brother is outside, sir."

Tommy looked up quickly with a frown.

"*What?!* There can't be three of you! What a calamity for the world!" shouted the cook, throwing his hands into the air. But why is he outside? He should be in here! I am strong, but he might spoil the appetites of Marie Antoinette and her consort."

Marie Antoinette and Louis the XVI were the camp pigs.

Theo started slowly toward the door.

"Hurry, hurry, lad!" The cook laughed loudly. "My appetite cannot be spoiled. I am a cook, you see."

Theo hurriedly opened the door and pulled Herman in by the collar of his coat.

The cook picked up a cleaver and looked fiercely at the trembling Herman.

"Why are you here? Why are you not in school?"

"Please, sir, the teacher was called to jury duty."

"Aha! Justice will be thwarted again!" He put down the cleaver and Herman breathed once more.

"Now, be it understood that he who enters my kitchen must do two things. Work and eat. You are no exception." He handed Herman a worn but lethal knife. Herman took it gingerly. The cook pointed silently to the table where Tommy worked. Herman joined him and picked up a fish. The boys all worked quietly for some time, Theo filling the wood boxes, Tommy and Herman cleaning the fish.

The morning went very slowly. The smells of bread, frying potatoes, thick bean soup, and apple pies were so strong that sometimes Tommy thought he might faint and Herman had to wipe his mouth on his sleeve several times. Now and then the cook glanced at them humorously and smiled to himself.

The noon whistle blew finally and within minutes the long, stuffy mess hall was half-full of loggers, steam rising from their mackinaws, their beards dripping melting snow onto the table tops. Those who worked near enough to the camp came in for the noon meal, while the cook's regular helpers carried lunch out to the lumberjacks working farther away in the woods.

The men were quiet as they ate, but a couple finished quickly and sat with their hands around heavy mugs of coffee. Alf Blucher sat near the end of a table across from the three Escher brothers, who were eating their way through a second plate of thick bean soup.

"Well, boys," Alf began loudly, "seen those bear tracks agin this morning." He winked broadly at Thoreau Mitchel, who sat down at the table next to Theo. Thoreau looked at Alf without smiling and went back to his apple pie.

145

"Musta been eight feet tall"

"Yep, musta been eight feet tall, from the look o' the tracks. Followin' sumpin'." He paused and took a large gulp of coffee. Herman had stopped eating and was staring apprehensively at the man. Theo and Tommy paid no attention but went on eating, cleaning their bowls with thick pieces of bread.

"Don't know what it coulda been he was a-followin'.
Bears don't generally follow . . . folks." He spoke the
last word quietly. "Not 'less they're crazed, o' course."

Herman put down his spoon.

Around the table there was a movement and several
of the men pushed back their plates and their cups and

moved toward the door. In a few minutes it would be time to return to work. Herman continued to look at Alf.

"Come on, Alf," said Thoreau impatiently, " 'bout time to get back."

"Hold it, hold it," replied Alf, and held up his hand. "Yep," he went on in a conversational voice, "musta been a crazed bear." Gulp of coffee. "Awful lotta blood." Herman gasped. Alf looked at him in mock surprise. "Sorry, boy, didn't know I'd scare you."

Thoreau grabbed Alf's arm and brought him to his feet. Alf was snickering and Thoreau said, "Don't pay him no mind, boy." He steered Alf toward the door, where they disappeared into the dreary cold forest beyond.

"Herman, don't listen to Alf," laughed Theo.

"But . . ." whimpered Herman.

"Listen, ninny, all the bears are asleep now, you know that," said Tommy. "Besides there aren't many around here now."

"Well . . ." said Theo, less confidently, "at least, nobody sees many."

"Alf did. He just said so," said Herman firmly.

"He made all that up," said Theo.

"How do you know?" asked Herman.

" 'Cause it doesn't make sense, that's how. If there was a bear, he'd be sleeping."

"Not if he was crazy," said Herman triumphantly, putting his spoon on the table with a firm bang.

"Oh, don't bother with him, Theo," said Tommy, "anybody who'd believe that. . . ." Tommy left his sentence unfinished and, taking his own plate and cup into the kitchen, started to help clear the mess hall.

Theo and Herman followed in a few minutes and all

three boys helped the regular kitchen helper finish cleaning the dining room.

"Does Mrs. Brownlow know where you are?" asked Theo, as together the three boys scrubbed the long tables.

"Sure," said Herman, "I told her I wouldn't be back till supper, that I was gonna go home with you for a while."

"Good," said Tommy in a pleased voice.

That afternoon, as the sun almost touched the horizon, the brothers started through the woods on the long hike home. Before they reached their own farmyard, the sun had disappeared and a bright half-moon, with the help of the snow-covered road, lighted the way into the little cabin.

The boys ate a hurried supper and then Theo urged Herman to start back to the Brownlows. Herman seemed reluctant to start and Theo felt guilty at hurrying him.

"You must go now, Herman," he said crossly.

"Oh, it isn't late," said the boy.

"You should get along, you know," said Tommy cheerfully.

"Oh, all right, but. . . ."

"What is it?" asked Theo, handing his brother his scarf and jacket.

"Oh, nothing," said Herman, slowly pulling on his mittens.

"There's plenty of light," said Theo, "just be sure to follow the Flat Road and don't take any short cuts."

When he was bundled into his wraps, Herman stood for some time at the door before he opened it. Theo, feeling worse by the minute, finally opened the door for him and propelled him into the cold outdoors.

149

"Theo. . ." began Herman, holding the door open with his shoulder.

"What, what?" said Theo.

"When can I come back home?"

"Soon, I hope, very soon," Theo answered.

"Good-bye," said Herman, and turned toward the road. The streak of light from the door disappeared.

Herman trotted slowly toward the road. When he reached it, he stopped for a minute, looking at the trees that seemed to loom as thickly as if no logger's axe had ever thinned them. Taking a deep breath, he started to run steadily up the road to Antrim.

The moonlight took the color from everything. Herman glanced at his red mittens, pumping rhythmically at his sides, and saw that they were dark grey now. The light played other tricks and he saw holes turn into humps and mounds changed to pits. The wind was curiously still tonight and Herman missed its garrulous and pushy company.

Whooosh!

The hairs on Herman's neck bristled and he stopped and turned quickly toward the sound, his eyes round. He saw, near the edge of the road, a tall pine, its upper branches still nodding gently and its burden of snow still sifting quietly down through the lower branches to the ground beneath. Herman's breath exploded from his chest and he laughed nervously. He turned and continued running.

In one place the road was very narrow and trees grew at its very edge. As he ran toward this narrow gap, Herman's pace grew slower and slower. He stopped and looked fearfully ahead. As he stood there, he heard a distant rustling behind him, then a thump he could feel through the soles of his sturdy black boots.

150

"He's coming!" whispered Herman and started running again.

He ran very fast now, passing through the narrows of the road so quickly he left branches bowing and dancing behind him.

While he ran, he could not hear the rustling and the thumping. At first, this comforted him and then he be-

"He's coming!"

gan to be fearful that his enemy was doing something behind his back, under cover of his pounding footsteps. He stopped suddenly and with great effort held his searing breath in his agonized lungs. Not a sound for seconds and then another snapping, as of twigs, and Herman was off again.

He passed Leander's hut and thought for a moment of stopping there to ask for help, and he actually slowed his footsteps, but as he did, he heard a sharp crack somewhere near the cabin.

"He's waiting for me there," he thought with panic and ran at full speed again.

Soon, his sides ached and each breath sent hot irons through his chest. He must rest. He saw, in the middle of the road, a short log, dropped and never picked up by a careless yard crew. When he reached it, he dropped full length upon it. In a few minutes, his breath came more easily and he sat up in order to look around.

The scene was peaceful and very still. The moon-made shadows were sharp and very black. Herman dropped his head into his hands for a second and sobbed a few times. Then it came again, the silent but earth-trembling thumps. They seemed to rattle the solid log on which Herman sat as if it were a matchstick. The boy rose quickly and started his headlong journey again.

At last he came to the turnoff for Antrim and he gratefully let the tears come as he sighted the lights in the hotel and the barbershop and heard laughter from the Methodist church where the young people were having their usual Friday night meeting.

The clatter of Herman's steps on the snow-covered logs of the road slowed to a walk as he reached the tiny parsonage beside the Baptist church.

"Herman, I was beginning to worry," said Mrs. Brownlow placidly as Herman came through the kitchen door.

She was washing beans through her fingers into a large brown crock and the thought of the baked beans tomorrow helped to cheer Herman.

"Yes'm. I ran as fast as I could," he said, self-righteously.

Mrs. Brownlow looked at him. "Why, child, no need to kill yourself. You'd of got here sooner or later, just walkin'."

"Yes'm." Herman took off his scarf, jacket, mittens, and other wraps and hung them near the stove on a low hook.

"Bedtime, now," said Mrs. Brownlow and, wiping her hands on her apron, shooed Herman on his way to bed.

Herman dreamed wildly of bears that night and the next day when his brothers came to see him, and to buy their supplies, Herman told Tommy the story of his wild run the night before. Tommy laughed unsympathetically, so Herman decided against telling Theo and asked Tommy not to tell either. Tommy promised reluctantly.

Instead, Herman told Jamie McDavitt, who was only six, behind the schoolhouse during a game of hide-and-seek. Jamie went straight home for supper and his mother remarked gratefully on his improved behavior.

14
Goodbye to Loggin'!

"It's pretty close to breakup," said Theo, "we should think about clearing the field at the north end of the pasture."

Tommy shivered inside his wrappings of quilts and old scarves. The early March wind made spring feel years away. The boys were walking home from North Camp late in the afternoon. The sun was still sending its bleakly cold rays from above the trees, but before the boys reached their house, the shadows would be stretched across their path.

"Why think of that now?" asked Tommy.

"Because we ought to write to Cousin 'Dolf." Theo spoke bravely.

"Write to 'Dolf! But you didn't think there was any use, that he wouldn't come!"

"We've got to ask him. Otherwise, well, otherwise

. . . . We've got to ask him, that's all." Theo spoke with finality.

Tommy started to speak and then looked at his brother's set face. Instead, he pushed his hands further into his pockets and walked in silence for a moment. He spoke again.

"How are we going to write to him? We hardly know our letters."

"Well, Herman does. He can help."

"All right," said Tommy, suddenly enthusiastic, "we'll ask him tomorrow."

"What shall I say?"

The next day was only Wednesday, but now that it was light until after supper, Herman came in the middle of the week, too, to help his brothers with such things as laundry and bread-making. His brothers considered him an expert in these matters. So, when Herman arrived after school and found his brothers sitting at the table, Theo carefully smoothing a small piece of rough paper and Tommy sharpening a stub of carpenter's pencil, he was surprised.

"Why aren't you working?" he said.

"We got the afternoon off — they don't care much now — because there's something important to do," said Theo impressively.

156

Herman quickly piled his mittens, boots, and collection of scarves and old sweaters on a bench near the fireplace, and joined his brothers at the table.

"We want you to write a letter," said Tommy.

Herman looked at his brother without expression.

"Cousin 'Dolf. We want him to know when we plan to start clearing the north pasture lot and we want him to come help us."

"Well. I guess I could do that. You could help, Tommy. You learned your letters last summer, when you broke your leg."

"All right, let's go," said Tommy impatiently.

Herman took the pencil from Tommy and carefully licked the point. He bent over the paper and then looked up.

"What shall I say?"

"Dear Cousin . . . ,"began Theo.

For an hour the boys struggled over the note. When they finally finished, they folded it carefully, and looked proudly at the outside of the square of paper. Slowly Theo's face lost its glow of happiness and his forehead creased with worry.

"Well? How do we get it to him?"

"I don't know. Can't we take it to the post office?"

"I guess so, but I think you have to pay to send letters."

"How much?" asked Herman.

Theo shrugged.

"We'll find out tomorrow."

The next day, when they finished work, Theo and Tommy went into Antrim instead of home. They went to the tiny post office in the front of the feed store and asked about mailing their precious note. They found that, since no boats were operating, it would take two or three weeks for their letter to reach Cousin 'Dolf. Theo was worried, but Tommy felt quite proud that they had thought to write him in enough time.

Spring came swiftly, once started. A strip of dark blue water dotted with pieces of ice appeared on the lake one day. Every day it grew wider and bluer as the ice moved farther out. The beach, not yet smoothed by the constant hand of the lake, was drifted with strange humps and windrows of sand. When, at last, the huge, sand-covered hills of ice that stood a little way out from the beach had melted, the spring storms would help the water again shape the beach into a smooth and mannerly shore.

Herman came home every day now, and often stayed the night. He helped the boys mend fences and clean the debris of winter from the farmyard.

One day, as the boys came home from the lumber camp, where the spring drive was almost under way, they found Herman's clothes and other possessions piled at the foot of the ladder leading to the loft.

Theo looked at him questioningly.

"Well, Mrs. Brownlow said it was all right. I can get to school all right," said Herman hesitatingly, "and I can't very well help much, if I'm stuck there in Antrim," he finished.

"That's fine," said Tommy gruffly. "Cousin 'Dolf should be here soon and so we can always use an extra hand."

Theo smiled at Tommy and then at Herman. They were together again.

"We'll have to quit after the drive, Tom," said Theo. "We'll quit at the same time the other farmers do."

The next few weeks were exciting ones for the boys. A long log drive was started down Torch Lake, where the logs had to be pulled by steam vessels in huge clumps down to the head of the Torch River. From there the

158

river itself carried them into Round Lake and, pushed from behind across the small lake, the logs piled through the narrows into Elk Lake and then were pulled to the town of Elk Rapids, where they were loaded by awkward cranes into the ships that went to Chicago.

Logging was not easy in Antrim County. There was no broad, rushing river to carry the lumber from the woods down to the harbors. Most of the lumber cut during the winter was sent to the beaches near Antrim. It was stacked on racks in small yards at the top of the bluff. When spring came and it was time to load the lumber, the racks were torn down and the logs pushed over the bluff to roll and scatter to the beach below.

One time Theo and Tommy rode down to the mouth of the Clam River on the cook's wangan. Most of the way they peeled potatoes, but from the deck of the flat boat that followed the drive crews they could see everything.

The Clam River was fast, though not very long. It entered Torch Lake with a rush and in the spring its white waters were filled with crashing logs. To the boys, used to the placid-seeming movement of the logs down the lake, it looked chaotic.

"Look! He'll go under!" shouted Tommy, clutching a potato in each hand.

"No, look," said Theo calmly, "he knows what to do."

The small, stringy-looking man in the red shirt they had been watching stepped smoothly from one rolling log to another, dodging a small cluster of logs, their ends in the air, that threatened to knock him down. As the cluster passed, he poked at it casually with his cant hook, a long-handled hook, and the cluster melted smoothly back into the even sea of logs. He stood effortlessly now, watching and waiting, riding past the boys. The wangan

159

was anchored in a backwater just north of the river mouth.

The sun warmed their backs as they worked and the spray sent up by the rolling mass of lumber cooled them now and then or spit on the compact iron stove the cook tended with great good humor. The rush of water and crash of lumber became part of them and they no longer noticed its mighty noise. They found they could speak in low voices and be heard better than if they screamed.

The small steam tug that pulled the lumber down the lake, once the logs had slowed and were becalmed on the lake, passed now and then, adding a bossy toot to the excitement of the moving logs. The boys waved whenever it passed.

Adding a bossy toot

This drive lasted only two days and at last the final dinner was served to the loggers and the boys had helped wash the pots and clean the stove. When they had almost finished, the tug pulled alongside, and while the cook shouted many heroic threats at her crew, the tug took the wangan in tow and started up the lake toward home.

The boys took their wages as they stepped onto the pier at Eastport and with much hesitation told the cook they would have to leave his employ.

"Why? I beat you too much, perhaps?" he asked with a fierce look. "Not enough? That is it! Not enough! Aha!"

He waved a large wooden spoon above his head.

"Oh, no, Mr. George . . . but. . . ."

"I pay you too much," he whispered, "and you think it unfair to the others."

"Oh . . . it's . . . well, we have to plant potatoes," stammered Tommy.

"*Potatoes!!!*" He laughed long.

"Yessir," said Theo, "you have been very good to us, and we want to thank you."

"*Potatoes???* But here you do not even need to plant them! Look!" and he pointed to two bushel baskets that stood, still full of potatoes, on the deck of the wangan.

"Yessir, I know."

"Farmers, phah!" said George, and flapped his apron wildly. "Here, to show you what I think of farmers and potatoes, I will make you cart those away before you can quit my generous employ." He gestured to the baskets.

Theo and Tommy grinned and blushed with delight.

"Yessir, thank you, sir, thank you."

"We'll come back next year," said Tommy kindly.

"Next year, haha! You will have no time! You will be

neck deep in filthy corn and potatoes. *Potatoes!* Hah!" He walked up the pier toward the lumber company office. He turned and waved his hand as the boys started awkwardly down the road with their baskets of potatoes.

When they reached home with their burdens, it was after dark and Herman was sitting nervously by the fire, his supper dishes already washed and put away.

"Hasn't he come?" asked Tommy with disappointment.

"No, he hasn't. What's that you're dragging?" said Herman.

Tommy and Theo told him the story of their two days at the river drive. They hurried through the recital, but they knew they would get nothing from Herman until they had told their tale. As they finished, Theo said, "Well, has there been a letter?"

"No. And I went in to town just this morning to find out. Nothing. And the *Sunnyside* was in, too, the day before."

The boys stood silently, disappointment clouding their faces.

"Well," said Theo, starting to move his basket into a corner. "It's still early. We'll go ahead and begin clearing the north lot tomorrow."

"Alone?"

"Sure, Herman. Cousin 'Dolf may not even write. He may just come. Probably will." Theo went on working. Tommy joined him now and in a few minutes the baskets were sitting neatly in a corner, a piece of sacking over them.

Herman moved now.

"Tomorrow we'll put them in sacks and put them in the barn," he said.

The boys spoke little as they climbed the ladder, and

after undressing they crawled into their pallets.

Tommy and Herman fell asleep quickly, but Theo lay wakefully for a few minutes.

"He'll come, I know he'll come," he whispered at last and then turned over to sleep.

The next day the boys started clearing the north lot. The job before them was large and difficult, but Theo and Tommy felt relief and even joy at being able to give all their time to the farm again. They were eager to attack the task vigorously.

The north lot was a good-sized piece of land that Jacob had wanted to use for growing beans, even though many people had told him beans would not grow well in this county. He knew something of growing beans and thought he could do it. Theo, Tommy, and Herman knew his wishes and so they had started to fulfill them as best they could.

The land was overrun with a second growth of jack pine, most no more than two or three feet high, and blackberry brambles that sent their runners underground so that one small bush seemed to be part of a monstrous sleeping giant.

Mornings were still cold. The skies were overcast. The afternoons grew warmer and when the sun shone, it was almost hot. The work was hard on their clothes and on their hands and legs. The blackberries, no matter how the boys crept up on them, always managed to grab the boys at some point where it would hurt or tear the most. The little pines were oozing sap, and each time the boys cut one their hands became a little stickier.

Tommy worked with an ancient grub, hacking at the everlasting blackberry roots. Theo cut down the little pines, and then dug and hacked out, as best he could, their stumps. Herman carried the cuttings to a pile be-

163

side the pasture fence. This had been a forest of mixed hemlocks, beech, and maple, with a small pine forest at one edge. When the hardwoods, and then the hemlock, and then the pine had been cut, the pine seedlings had taken over. The ground was spongy from the centuries of leaves and needles that had lain under the trees when the forest existed. Now, after the snows had melted and the rains had drenched it day after day, this spongy soil sent little puddles into their shabby boots.

Near noon, Herman went down through the pasture to the house and brought back a lunch of bread, milk, and apples. The apples had only barely lasted through the winter and these were withered and small. They were still sweet though, and smelled of autumn and harvests.

In the afternoon a cold rain started. The boys huddled against the pile of little pine trees that Herman had stacked. Their jackets were soon soaked through. None of them had worn their scarves or quilt mufflers and soon they were very cold. Finally, however, the rain stopped and the spring sun came through brilliantly. The boys crawled gratefully out of their shelter and, picking up their tools, went on with their work.

The sun grew warmer and warmer. At last the three boys took off their jackets and spread them to dry on the rails of the fence that ran along the north side of the pasture. The fence was only half built and it was only because of the thick underbrush on the east side of the pasture that the cow did not roam farther than she did. As it was, sometimes Tommy had to go half a mile or more into the scrub growth before he found her.

Finally Theo looked at the sun low in the west and decided that it was time to stop for the day. The boys gathered their tools and jackets and climbed the fence. When they reached the other side, Theo stopped and Tommy and Herman paused with him. They looked back at the field they had been working in since early morning.

"Why," said Tommy in surprise, "it doesn't look as if we'd done anything!"

"It doesn't, does it?" There was deep weariness in Theo's voice.

"We'll do more tomorrow," said Herman, "and pretty soon we'll be able to see. . . ."

". . . and Cousin 'Dolf will surely be here soon," said Tommy grimly, reaching down to rub his aching leg.

15
An Indian Messenger

The April day was one of meetings and comings and
goings.

Usually, the boys saw no one for days on end, unless
they made a trip to town. Sometimes Leander came by
with a string of smelt or some early mushrooms, but he
didn't stay long. Sometimes the boys didn't know he had
been there until after he had gone. They had each other
for company and the work of the small farm kept them
busy without rest from morning until night.

But today was different. Herman felt restless as he
fixed breakfast. He slapped the tin plates onto the table
with more than the usual clanking.

"Don't be so noisy," said Tommy.

"Nothing but bread and milk again?" asked Theo.

Herman said nothing, folding his lips very tightly together.

"Here's some butter," offered Tommy.

"Isn't there any coffee?" asked Theo.

"No," said Herman.

The boys ate in silence for a few minutes and then they heard, very close to the front door, snuffling and scratching that seemed to be several animals.

Herman and Tommy ran together and pulled open the door. Two half-grown dogs floundered into the room and, snuffling and panting, made one circuit of the room. When they reached the door again, they answered a shrill whistle from the yard. The three boys stepped out after the dogs and saw, leaning against a tree near the door, a tall young Indian. He was dressed in buckskin pants and a soft, colorful wool shirt. His hair was neatly trimmed and combed beneath a yellow felt wide-brimmed hat. He grinned at the boys as they came out.

"You the Eschers?" he asked.

Theo nodded. Herman was squatting down, rubbing the ears of one of the dogs.

"Got a message from you cousin."

"From 'Dolf?"

"Yeh. He say he can't come. Not this year. He got good job in sled factory. Me, too. He can't stop to help you farm."

The young man looked at each of the brothers in turn, still smiling.

"Not coming?" echoed Tommy weakly.

Herman looked angrily at the ground before him.

"What'll we do?" asked Tommy.

"We'll . . . we'll just have to go ahead ourselves," answered Theo.

Herman looked at three long scratches on the back of one hand and then at the tears and rips in his trousers.

The Indian stopped smiling now and was watching the boys closely.

168

"I'm sorry," he said finally.

Theo looked at him in surprise.

"How much you pay? I could help."

"We couldn't pay anything," said Theo, "we hardly have enough for ourselves. In a while, we won't have that," he finished with a snort.

"I'm sorry. I can't work for nothing. I got a ol' mother to feed."

The boys looked at him again, puzzlement in their faces.

"But *you* don't have to do anything for us. We're not your relatives."

"We thank you anyway," said Tommy, with a wavering smile.

"We could give you some bread and milk for your trouble," said Theo.

The Indian hesitated, looking for a moment at the three worried faces before him. Then he motioned up the road and said, "I gotta go on. Not today, thanks." He whistled for his dogs, waved at the boys and went up the road toward Antrim.

The three were very still for several minutes. The sun was bright in a clear blue sky. Little breezes hummed through the tall pines, singing today, not sighing.

"Come on," said Theo in a hard voice, "we gotta sharpen the axe before we start today."

He went into the cabin and returned with his axe, while Tommy pulled on one end of an old grindstone that sat near the wall of the house. When he had it far enough out so that Theo could straddle the seat, he started to turn it for his brother. Herman had fetched a dipper of water from the well and slowly poured it on the stone as Theo held the axe blade carefully against the turning stone. Several minutes passed, the spark now and then adding only a little glimmer to an already shining day. At last Theo got up, silently. His brothers pushed the wheel back up against the house and Herman hung the dipper near the well again.

"I'll get the saw and grub hoe," said Tommy, running toward the barn.

Theo and Herman walked after him on the way to the north lot.

"We must finish tomorrow," Theo said fiercely. "We have planting to begin."

Just then they heard the creaks, clatter, and slow pounding that meant a wagon was coming up the Flat Road. The boys stopped and waited a moment where they could see the part of the road that passed their front yard. Pretty soon it came in sight. It was piled high with household goods, tools and pots hanging over the sides. A woman in a sun bonnet sat in the driver's seat, two children beside her. Walking at the horses' heads were two men. Theo could see that one of them was Rev. Brownlow. The minister looked their way as the wagon moved slowly by. He said something to the man walking with him and in a second the team had stopped. Theo and Herman, joined now by Tommy, walked toward the gate of the yard.

"Hello, boys!" called Rev. Brownlow, "come here a minute, if you can."

The brothers walked out to the road.

"Like to have you meet your new neighbors," said Rev. Brownlow. "Boys, this is Mr. and Mrs. Jansen Hanson, and Emil and Frances."

"How do you do, sir," said Theo, shaking hands with Mr. Hanson.

"These are the Escher boys I was telling you about."

"Howdy, lads." Mr. Hanson was tall, broad-shouldered,

and very blond. His tanned skin looked almost like a mask around the pale blue of his eyes. He spoke with a smile and shook hands heartily with the three brothers. Mrs. Hanson and the children nodded and smiled from the wagon.

"The Hansons got the eighty acres south of your creek," said Rev. Brownlow.

"Oh," said Herman. "Well, it's all burned over for you."

"I know. That's too bad, but it didn't get the whole place, some of it's still all right."

Theo and Tommy looked curiously at Rev. Brownlow. He laughed.

"Mr. Hanson thinks like Leander, that the burning kills something in the earth. He's going to plant cherry trees, boys."

"Oh," said the boys politely.

"Yep. Only I was countin' on unburned land. It'll be thin goin' for longer than I'd counted. Well, glad to have met you boys. Got to be gettin' on." He flapped the reins over the horses' backs and started walking slowly beside them again.

"Glad to have met you boys"

Rev. Brownlow stayed with the brothers for a minute.

"Be with you in a minute, Mr. Hanson," he called after the farmer and then turned to the boys.

"You boys don't look any too happy this morning. Can I help?"

"No, sir, thank you," said Theo.

"Cousin 'Dolf can't come," said Herman. The other two looked at him with anger.

"I'm sorry, boys. I hope you weren't counting too much on his help."

"No, sir, well, yes, sir, I guess we were. Too much," said Tommy.

"We're trying to clear the north lot. It's hard and we should be plantin' too," said Herman.

"We're almost out of flour again, and we spent all our money for seed. . . ," said Tommy.

". . . 'cause our seed potatoes went bad. Papa knew how to keep them, but I guess we don't," finished Herman.

"Things aren't as bad as they make it sound, sir," said Theo. He looked straight at the minister as he went on, "We have a lot to do, that's true, but we'll get it done. I remember how Papa did things and I'll see that they get done."

"But it's a long time 'til harvest. Can you hold out all summer?" asked Rev. Brownlow gently.

"We'll manage." Theo looked at his brothers. In spite of his words, their faces were still worried and pinched.

"We'll have to go to work someplace else again," blurted Tommy.

"But how can we?" asked Herman. "There's the corn to hoe *and* the potatoes . . . let alone ever gettin' the

172

north lot cleared *and* planted in *beans!"* He banged the ground with the hoe he carried.

The boys were talking to each other now and Rev. Brownlow stood quietly. They were making decisions now, decisions that might have waited until evening, if the subject hadn't come up then.

"Where would we work?" asked Theo flatly.

"On the beach, of course, where else?" replied Tommy.

"I'm still not big enough," said Herman, "but I could stay home and hoe potatoes and corn. Some potatoes and some corn," he added practically.

"That's not running a farm," warned Theo.

"No. . . ," Tommy started, but realized he had no answer.

"Boys. . . ," Rev. Brownlow began. They looked at him, almost startled that he was still there.

"Never mind, for now. I'm sorry, boys, that you're having trouble. You know I am here to help you if you need it."

"Thank you, sir," said Tommy. He felt a strange gratitude that this man was interested in them.

Rev. Brownlow started down the road after the disappearing wagon, going at a steady trot. He waved over his shoulder at the three boys.

"Well, what'll we do?" asked Herman, continuing their conversation.

"Let's clear the north lot now," said Theo, shouldering his axe and starting in that direction.

His brothers followed without a word.

The day was very warm and still. Insects were beginning to add their tiny conversations to the voices of nature and the windless plot was filled with their sound today. The boys worked steadily through the morning,

173

and the pile of small trees and blackberry brambles grew. At noon, when Herman had returned with their lunch, the three walked farther back into the woods and sat in the scanty shade of two six-foot-high pine trees.

Herman scratched frantically at a spot between his shoulder blades and Tommy pulled the legs of his pants above his knees, as he sat with his back against a giant log. Automatically he began to rub his leg. Theo munched thoughtfully at a ragged hunk of bread.

"Tomorrow, Tom," he began, "we will go to the Company and ask for jobs. Herman will stay home and tend to the farm." There was uncertainty in his voice as he said the last words.

"Tomorrow," said Tommy and nodded gravely.

They rested a little while after their lunch and then, wearily picking up their axes and hoes, went back to the task of clearing the north lot.

16
Britches and Rain

Now the boys waited for a whistle up the bay. The lumber company cut down the wood and brought it to the harbors and beaches, but it was up to each ship captain, looking for a cargo, to see that the lumber was loaded onto his vessel. So whenever a ship came into the bay and wanted a cargo of timber, its whistle would blow in a certain pattern and men who wanted work would come to do the loading.

Theo and Tommy worked from the late spring and all through the summer. Some days there would be no work and on those days, together with Herman, they planted and tended their meager crops. Unable to grub out all of the stumps in the north lot, they had planted turnips and beans among the snags. Other days, when there was no work at the beach or on the pier, they helped their new neighbor, Mr. Hanson, cut up the two large trees he had bought from them. Theo and Tommy

*The ships came in as close
as they safely could*

swung on one end of the crosscut saw and Mr. Hanson
on the other.

Most of their time was spent on the pier or on the
beach, though. At first, they worked on the pier loading shingles. During the winter, many men and boys
had spent their days cutting these shingles and now they
lay tied in bundles, stacked in huge piles, waiting to be
carried to Chicago. The boys could load shingles without too much trouble and they enjoyed working on the
pier so close to the ships. Even the most wind-battered
old schooner was exciting and adventurous in their eyes,
and they remembered their father's tales of their own

sea-crossing as they pushed another bundle of sweet-smelling shingles onto the littered deck of a weary old sailing vessel.

Working on the beach was a different matter. The work was heavy and they were expected to do their share; no one relieved them of an extra-heavy plank, or offered to load their share of posts. And they did not ask for favors. They knew, also, without thinking of it really, that this was a man's work, and they were eager to accept a man's position in this community.

Loading heavy timber from the beach was not easy. The ships came in as close as they safely could, but this still left several hundred feet of water between the logs and their destination. Before the lumber reached the beach, it had been roughly cut in different sizes. Some of it had been cut into short lengths for railroad ties and fence posts; some of the lumber was simply cut into manageable lengths which would be sold as cord-wood. Sometimes the lumber was loaded as planks, two inches thick and twelve feet long, which had been cut at the mill in Antrim and floated the short way up the beach to the loading area. Still undried and heavy with sap, these boards were heavier than they looked. Carrying his end, Tommy often felt sharp twinges in his leg.

Cordwood and planks were loaded onto scows — large, flat-bottomed boats — and pulled out to the vessel. The pulling was tedious and difficult. A length of rope ran from the front of the scow, out to the ship, through a metal loop on the ship's bows, and then back to shore. By pulling on the rope, two men on the beach could move the scow out to the ship. Winches and cranes were used to load the contents of the scow into the ship's hold.

The smaller pieces, railroad ties and posts, were floated
out to the ship. A kind of floating fence of large logs
was built in the water and the railroad ties and posts
were tossed into this enclosure. This boom was floated
out to the vessel. Men on rafts used their picaroons to
load this wood onto the vessel. A picaroon was a kind
of axe with a hook where the blade would usually be.
The tallest, strongest men were usually used for this
work; it was a long way from the boom up and over
the rail of a ship.

Herman was faithful to his duties, too, and every day
he brought lunch to his brothers on the beach.

The noon whistle blew one day, just as Herman appeared over the bluff and started sliding down the sandy
track to the beach below. As he reached the bottom,
the men had dropped their tools and started to open
and eat their own lunches.

Theo and Tommy stood watching the lunches their
fellow workers had opened. They could smell the ham
and the cheese, the apple pie and ginger cookies. Some
of the men carried meat pies, wrapped in many layers of
paper, still steaming just enough to make Tommy's
mouth water uncontrollably.

"Here," said Herman, pulling at his brother's sleeve,
"here's your lunch!"

"Oh," said Tommy, turning quickly, "I didn't see
you." He grabbed the small packet Herman held out
to him.

"I said it three times," said Herman crossly. "Well,
aren't you going to sit down and eat it?"

"Yes, yes, sure," said Theo slowly, "but let's go over
there." He pointed to a place up the beach, away from
the crowd of workers. A piece of driftwood lay with its
end in the water. They walked to the log and sat down

178

together, their backs to the jumbled pile of lumber that lay waiting on the beach.

The lunch they opened was simple: there was a piece of bread for each boy, a small piece of dried fish, and a careful handful of wild strawberries in a tin cup. Tommy looked at it and and sighed heavily. Theo frowned at him fiercely and Tommy cleared his throat hastily.

"No eggs today, huh?"

"No. We ate them all yesterday." Herman tore a piece of fish with his teeth.

"Well, say, that's too bad. I always like a nice *hard-* boiled egg." Theo laughed as Tommy spoke. Herman continued to eat with quiet dignity. Tommy had been poking fun at his brother because Herman had once boiled some eggs so long that the yokes had turned blue.

Tommy dipped his bread in the water and held it there a minute or two. Theo watched him and then did the same. The bread was very hard. At home, they soaked it in milk so that they could chew it, or sometimes in maple syrup, but here, only the waters of the bay were offered to soften their bread.

The boys ate in silence for a while and then turned as they heard footsteps behind them. Alf Blucher was shambling toward them across the sand. Tommy let out a small hissing sound. Theo kicked his brother under cover of the log. Sitting very still, the three watched him come.

Alf seemed smaller in the summer and very untidy. He had no children and the boys had thought this was just as well, because if he had had, the children would have led lives of the deepest misery. Herman was still trying to live down the imaginary bear chase of the winter before.

"Hi, you boys! Eatin' hearty, I guess," he called before he reached them. Belching loudly, he continued toward them. "Had to throw away a half a fried chicken, I did!" he shouted again. "My wife just don't know when to stop feedin' me." Before he could reach them, the whistle blew for a return to work and Alf turned hastily and trotted back to the work area.

Herman looked, with pain in his face, at the bit of bread he held.

"Don't listen to him," muttered Tommy, starting toward the half-loaded scow on which he was working.

"No," said Theo, patting Herman on the head, "his lunch is never any great shakes, believe it." Herman gave his older brother a half-smile.

"C'mon and watch a while," said Tommy.

"Oughta get home and hoe turnips," said Herman, but still he followed his brothers up the beach.

Theo and Tommy joined the men who were clustered around a stack of twelve-foot planks, jumbled and tossed on the beach when the rollways had been removed earlier in the spring. The pile looked as if a giant had carelessly flung down a handful of matches. They each grabbed the end of a plank held at the opposite end by one of the other men.

Herman walked more slowly up the beach behind them. He stood a little way up the bluff, back from the crowd of laboring men. He watched for a little while.

After several minutes, as he stood there, he noticed Alf talking to Enos Swickert and laughing as he pointed up the bluff. Herman realized quickly that Alf was pointing at him. Enos glanced once and then went on with his work, hoisting an end of a heavy green plank. Alf went to another of the men and continued his laughing in Herman's direction. Herman looked down at himself, perplexed, and then, reddening, he turned and

180

started up the bluff, scrambling as quickly as possible from one clump of beach grass to another.

He tried to shield himself from view as much as possible, because he knew now why Alf had laughed. His trousers were almost completely shredded. The weeks in the north lot, carrying and piling the brambles, had done the job; the small tears had become larger and each large tear even greater, until barely anything was left whole. He had grown so used to putting on these tatters each morning that he no longer was aware of how they must look to others. Now he understood and the back of his neck burned with shame. Dodging from tree to tree, he reached the cabin and bursting in, he flung himself to the floor. He hid his face and sobbed tightly once or twice.

Tommy dipped
his bread in the water

"Papa, Papa," he said over and over.

At last he lay still and then, finally, turned over. Sitting up, he looked closely at his pants and then fingered them indecisively. At last he slipped out of them and, carrying them, went to the corner cupboard. On a top shelf, toward the back, stood an ancient mending basket. The balls of thread within were dusty from lack of use, but Herman blew off the dust and, scrabbling in the bottom, managed to find a pin cushion. In the middle was a fat little emery ball and through this was stuck a needle.

For a long time Herman struggled with his trousers. First, the tedious time of threading the needle, which seemed to hate him personally. Then, the frustration of finding, after several starts, that the thread had to be knotted at the end. And, finally, the wilderness of darns and seams that must be made. Long before the whistle blew for the end of the working day on the beach, Herman had thrown the pants furiously into a corner. He sat for some time, tears running down his cheeks and dropping from his chin. There was no money for trousers. They were able to buy a few supplies, enough to keep themselves and their cow alive, and that was all. The few pennies that might be left over each week were saved carefully so that they could buy a new axe handle and a decent hay rake before summer came to an end.

At last, Herman smiled suddenly and sat up straight. He rushed to the corner where his trousers lay and, putting them on hurriedly, he ran from the cabin to the barn.

At one end of the barn was an unused horse stall. It was full of cobwebs and ancient hay. In one corner stood a large tin box that had once held biscuits. Herman pulled at the lid with all his strength. Finally it opened with a rattle and a squeak. A musty odor arose from the inside, but Herman reached in eagerly and pulled out the contents — a large, dark-red horse blanket.

He ran back to the cabin with his find and shook it out before going in. He spread it on the floor and looked at it thoughtfully for some time. At last he took off his tattered pants again and laid them carefully on the blanket. He smoothed them fussily and taking a large pair of tin shears that hung on the wall, he began to cut.

When Theo and Tommy arrived home that night, they found that Herman had done very little during the day and, with a couple of hours of daylight after supper, they took their hoes to the turnip field where they hacked at the weeds until dark. The older boys said very little as they trudged through the early summer evening back to the small house under the trees. Herman felt the accusation in their rounded shoulders and the weariness of their sighs as they finally slumped down on their mattresses and went to sleep. If Tommy and Theo could have seen his face in the dark, they would have seen a look of determination, however. He would continue with his project no matter what.

Two days later, as the noon whistle on the beach blew, Theo and Tommy as usual looked up to the bluff for their brother. Their chins dropped and their eyes stared as they saw Herman, taking long sliding strides, coming down the bluff in dark-red trousers.

"What . . . ?" said Tommy.

"Where . . . !" exclaimed Theo. Putting down the posts they were loading, they ran to their brother.

Herman stood proudly at the foot of the bluff, his hands on his hips — since he didn't know how to make pockets.

Theo and Tommy looked at him a minute, then Tom-

my poked Theo. They could see that the trousers had
lived a different life in a different form at one time.
They knew them well from another time.

"Ah . . . where, I mean, how . . . well, how did you do
it?" asked Tommy.

"I just did it, that's all," said Herman firmly, handing Theo the lunch and leading the way up the beach
to their favorite driftwood log. Theo and Tommy followed dazedly.

Without a further word, the boys sat down and Theo
parceled out the lunch. They ate for some time, listening
to the gulls, who seemed to have heard the noon whistle,
too, and hovered around the schooner anchored out
from shore. The birds seemed to feel that the food was
better, even just a little way out to sea. They wheeled
and cried and dived, their calling very sharp and clear
now that the donkey engine of the ship's winch was
silent for a while.

Herman swallowed the last of a piece of corn bread.

"Now he can't laugh at me," he announced.

"Laugh at you? Who?" asked Theo.

"Alf."

"Why?"

"Because of my other pants, o' course. There wasn't
a whole place left big enough to wipe my little finger."

Theo and Tommy looked at each other. They thought
of the long evenings hoeing turnips that Herman should
have hoed and corn that Herman should have weeded.
They sat for a minute and then Tommy said, "They're
nice britches. You did a good job." He went on eating
the dried apple he held.

Theo, too, went back to his lunch.

Herman grinned and jumping up found a handful

of flat stones and began to skip them over the gently moving waters of the bay.

Saturday was a long and busy day for the brothers. On Friday they had collected their pay from the mate of the ship they had been loading, and Saturday morning Theo went into town to buy supplies. He took Herman's old wagon, but sometimes even that was not big enough and he had to make two trips. Herman, who ruled the farm alone during the week, was not in charge on Saturday and did as Tommy told him to do. The mattresses were aired and the blankets hung outdoors to flap in the breeze. A small fire was built in the yard and a huge kettle placed on the fire and then filled with water. Another kettle beside it held cold water. Using the soft yellow soap that Theo had bought in town, Herman washed their clothes and hung them to dry. If it rained, he washed them miserably in cold water in the barn. Their clothes were so few that this job did not take long. When it was done, Herman made their week's supply of bread, trying desperately to remember everything that should go in it. He chopped wood, too. It seemed to him as if he were always chopping wood. The stack grew as he worked, but almost before the next day, it had shrunk and he must chop again.

During the morning, Tommy helped Herman when he could, but most of the time he spent cleaning the cow's stall, putting in fresh straw and scrubbing the cow herself with a brush. She did not like to be scrubbed and told him so loudly and often during the operation. Tommy also did whatever planting and cultivating he could during the morning.

One Friday night a chill wind was blowing, although it was now the end of June. The boys sat near the fire and Theo talked of the things that should be done the next day.

"We'll hoe the turnips and the beans, but we've got to find some more deadheads and bring them in for firewood."

"What we really oughta do is cut some maple and bring it down and let it dry for firewood, is what we oughta do," said Tommy grimly.

"Well, we can't. We haven't time. You know it." Theo hit his fist against the stones of the fireplace.

"I could go fishing with Leander," Herman offered.

"Who would that help?" said Tommy scornfully. "Nobody but you. Not even Leander."

"We could eat the fish I catch, is what," said Herman defiantly.

"You can't catch anything," sneered Tommy. Herman half stood and started to lunge at Tommy.

"Stop it!" ordered Theo. Herman sat down, grumbling.

"We haven't time for any of that, either." Theo went on telling his brothers what they would do the next day. At last they climbed wearily up the ladder to the loft and were soon in bed asleep.

The next morning, Tommy woke first and lay in bed a moment, listening.

"Oh, no!" he cried loudly, waking both Herman and Theo.

"What is't?" mumbled Theo.

"Listen," said Tommy.

"Oh, no!" echoed Theo after a moment.

"Well, I guess we can't do anything today," said Herman, and prepared to turn over and sleep some more.

The rain was loud and hard on the roof over their

186

heads. The sound was steady, too. It strummed above them without any change in its rhythm.

"No," said Theo, frantically throwing off the quilts and beginning to pull on his clothes, "no, we've got to work, no matter what. When will we do it, if we don't do it today?"

"Why not tomorrow," muttered Herman, not daring to speak out loud.

"You know why. We don't work on Sunday, that's all. Papa said it's the best rule any man can follow and especially a farmer," answered Theo.

By this time, all three boys were out of bed and half-dressed. In a few moments, Theo and Tommy were downstairs beginning to fix a simple breakfast.

"What about the beds?" called Herman from the loft.

"Well, spread the blankets out on the floor up there. We can put 'em outdoors later today, if the sun comes out. Otherwise, we'll just turn 'em over."

After breakfast, Theo started for Antrim. Before he had reached the road, his shoulders were soaked to the skin. Tommy had thrown an old blanket over his own shoulders when he had gone to milk the cow, but Theo would not be seen in town with such a thing. Tommy thought he was foolish, but Herman understood.

"We'll wash in the barn. Go get the clothes and come on," said Tommy. He found the soap in the corner cupboard while Herman went up the ladder.

"Tommy!" called Herman from the loft.

"What?"

"Is it wet down there?"

"Wet? Of course not!"

"Well, it will be soon, I guess. Right about the end of the table."

Tommy turned and stood at the end of the table. He

187

looked toward the ceiling and in a moment a drop of water fell on his forehead. In a moment three more fell, and then a small steady stream. He sighed. Turning toward the cupboard, he rummaged out a large, dusty soup pot and placed it under the drip. Then he ran up to where Herman stood in the loft.

Theo's mattress was soaked through in the middle. The blankets which were spread on the floor on the other side of the loft were still dry.

"It started while I stood here. It did, it really did."

Tommy examined the roof where the water was coming in. It came in a steady stream from outside, straight to a crack in the floor and down to the soup pot below. Tommy scratched his head.

"Well, bring Theo's mattress down. We'll put it by the fire. Guess the soup pot's in the best place now. No sense bringing it up here. Just have to carry it down the ladder to empty it." He sighed heavily again.

Herman and Tommy worked silently through the morning. The water was very cold in the wash kettle, the socks very dirty, the cow's stall unusually messy. The rain came down very hard, all the time.

At noon, Tommy and Herman ran back to the cabin, just as Theo arrived from town. The two went into a huddle around the fire, steam rising from their clothes. Herman and Tommy were silent when Theo began to unpack their supplies and put them away.

"What's this!" exclaimed Theo, noticing the soup pot at last.

"A leak in the roof," stated Tommy.

Theo stood for a long time, holding a basket of eggs. He looked at the ceiling and at the water coming down.

"Well, we got somethin' to do today, since we can't hoe the corn."

188

"What d'ya mean?" asked Tommy.

"We gotta make shingles and put 'em on soon's it dries out."

Herman looked at the shingle-maker, the schnitzel-bank, that stood in the far corner beside the fireplace. He smiled with satisfaction.

But Tommy was not reassured.

"Where do we get dry wood?" he asked.

"There are two cedar logs in the barn loft, cut up into the right lengths for making shingles. I found 'em last summer. Papa must have put them there to season." Then Theo led the way up to the loft to look more closely at the leak.

The boys huddled for a few minutes under the eaves, watching the stream of water being driven like a giant nail through their house. Then they climbed down the ladder. In a few minutes they were all ready to go to the barn.

There they climbed to the hayloft in search of the cedar logs. They found them in a dark corner, half covered with hay. They were larger than Theo had remembered and they would have to be cut before the boys could take any part of them down to be cut into shingles. Herman went back to the cabin for a saw, shielding it carefully with his coat as he returned through the rain.

The day crept on, with the loud drumming of the rain always around them. Tommy and Herman draped the wet washing around the cabin, where it added its irregular drips to the steady batter of the stream pouring through the loft. Theo struggled for hours with the schnitzelbank, at last mastering its tricky mechanism for holding the solid piece of wood while he carved a shingle. He had made a dozen shingles by suppertime and stacked them in a corner of the room and covered

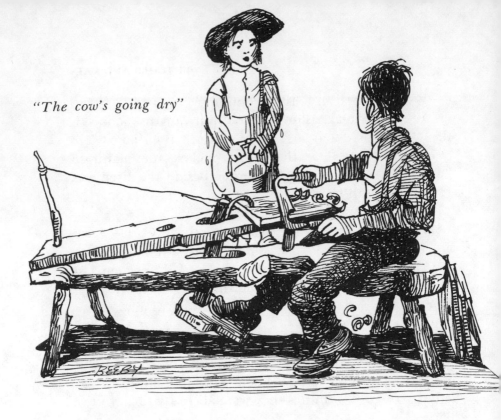

"*The cow's going dry*"

them with a piece of sacking. He would have to wait until the sun had dried the roof before he could put them over the leak.

Tommy came back from milking the cow with a look of consternation on his face.

"The cow's going dry, I think," he said.

Herman gasped and Theo groaned, "Oh, no!"

"Well, look," said Tommy, "this is all I got and it's been getting less, but I didn't want to worry you." He showed his brothers the pail, less than a quarter full of milk."

"In a day or two we won't get any," he finished and, covering the pail again, went out the door to lower the pail carefully into the well.

That evening the three boys sat wearily by the fire. They were silent for some time and then Theo uttered a cry and struck the floor angrily with both fists. Tommy shivered and Herman looked up in surprise.

"Nothing done today," said Theo, "nothing at all. Only twelve shingles. Twelve! Why, most men would make that many in an hour!"

"Not quite," murmured Herman.

"Well, almost!" shouted Theo. "And then the leak, and the cow, and nothing else done. No hoeing, no wood chopped, nothing." He put his head down on his knees and sighed deeply.

"What'll we do, Theo?" asked Tommy in a little voice. "We've got to work. You know we can't get by unless we do."

Theo shook his head without speaking.

When they crawled into their beds that night, clammy with the dampness of the day, each asked silently in his own way for the strength to go on and the knowledge to know how.

17
A Neighbor's Offer

Early Sunday morning, before Tommy had gotten up to milk the cow, Theo had left the cabin. He carried a piece of bread in one hand and in the other a cold potato, left from supper the night before.

The morning was lovely and fresh. The sun shone in a clear sky. Raindrops sparkled among the soft dark branches of the evergreens that rose around the little house. The birds had stopped their early morning song and were almost silent as they busied themselves finding breakfast. Theo munched his breakfast as he ambled slowly away from the house toward the stream that ran between their land and that of their neighbors, the Hansons. He liked the coolness among the red osiers that hung over the banks and today he wanted to think.

He finished his bread and potato just as Tommy rattled out of the house with his milk pail. The brothers could not see each other and Tommy did not know where Theo had gone.

As he came into the yard, Tommy called, "Theo! Theo, where are you?"

He listened for a moment and then hurried toward the barn. Theo did not answer. He could see the farmyard through the leaves. It was warm and clean today. The muddy dooryard was drying quickly in the sun and only a few clear pools stood here and there on the bare earth.

Theo's throat ached terribly as he struggled to keep the tears from his eyes. He wondered how they could keep their home, the home that Papa had lived and died for. He knew that if they could not farm their land, there would be nothing to eat next winter. They had no backlog at all. Until yesterday, he felt they had done well. They had kept together, they had proven to themselves that they could run their farm, feed and clothe themselves, that he and Tommy, at least, could hold men's jobs. Now, if they had to ask for help, Theo felt it would seem that they had failed.

Tommy was coming slowly across the farmyard, the pail swinging lightly from his hand. Theo could tell that it was empty, or nearly so.

"Hey!" he called and left the shelter of the osiers and came toward the house. He met Tommy near the door and looked casually into the pail.

"That's it, I guess," said Tommy decisively.

"Ummm," Theo answered and shook his head. There was only a cup or two of milk in the bottom of the pail.

"Come in, we're having eggs for breakfast!" called Herman.

Tommy and Theo went in and found Herman carefully turning six eggs that sputtered in the frying pan over the fire. The cabin was warm, even though it was early in the day. Herman put the frying pan on the middle of the table and put two eggs on each tin plate. The boys cut themselves hunks of bread and dipped them into the grease that remained in the frying pan. Herman smacked his lips.

"Maybe we could keep chickens," he ventured cheerfully.

"We'll be lucky to keep the farm. Remember, there's taxes, too. And we gotta pay those with money." Theo listlessly mopped his plate with the last of his bread.

Tommy stopped eating and looked gloomily at his older brother.

Just then there was a knocking at the door. The boys looked up to see Rev. Brownlow framed in the doorway. The door was open and the big man was rapping on the door frame.

"Good morning, boys! Beautiful sabbath, isn't it?"

The three boys rose quickly from the table and offered the minister a seat. Rev. Brownlow sat down.

"I can't stay, only a minute. I must get back for services, but I was passing and stopped to invite you all to dinner this afternoon. I have something to talk over with you."

The boys looked at each other. Herman smiled wanly. Tommy looked at Theo.

"We'd like to, sir. Thank you," he said.

195

"When should we come, sir?" put in Herman.

"Well, why don't you come a little bit after noon." He smiled wistfully. "I'd like to say come to church and then come to dinner, but I realize that would not be fair to my promises to your father." He rose, still smiling, and continued, "So, come right after noon."

"Yes, sir," said Tommy, walking with him to the door.

"Thank you, Rev. Brownlow," called Herman.

"What do you think he wants?" asked Tommy when the minister had gone and the brothers turned toward the table to clear away their breakfast.

"I don't know," said Theo, "I . . . well . . . I just don't know."

"Of course not," said Herman. "Let's wait 'till this noon."

Tommy nodded.

The boys spent the morning walking restlessly around the farm. Theo listed in his mind, as they walked, all the things that needed to be done. There were fences to mend, for one thing, and rabbits, deer, blackbirds, chipmunks, skunks, and blue jays were enjoying the tender new beans that had begun to appear in the wavy rows they had planted. They should be protected, but Theo couldn't figure out how to rig up a scarecrow, since they needed all their clothes. The stream needed cleaning badly in spots because the cow needed its water where it ran through a corner of the pasture at the bottom of the hill.

And, oh, the cow! What they would do about her, Theo had no idea. Now they didn't even have milk of their own and so they were entirely dependent upon their earnings for everything they ate.

Theo groaned. He thought of how much they needed their harvest and how little it would yield. He was careful, though, not to show his discouragement in front of Herman and Tommy.

That morning, almost an hour before noon, the three boys stood by the well without their shirts and washed themselves thoroughly with a handful of the yellow soap that Tommy and Herman used for washing clothes. The boys were red and shiny when they had finished, and their hair dripped placidly onto their brown shoulders. Theo brushed his hair carefully with an old hairbrush. When they were through washing and brushing their hair, they put on shirts that had been washed the day before. They were clean but had not been ironed, had never been ironed, in fact. There was nothing they could do about their old, soiled trousers, but brush them some, which they did. They had discarded shoes some weeks before and would think nothing more about them until the frosts began that fall. No one else would, either, and they knew that the younger of the minister's children would be barefoot also, even though it was Sunday. Theo looked at them critically before they set out. He didn't know exactly what he was looking for when he looked them over, but they seemed to be clean and he felt this mattered most. He gave his approval and the three started up the Flat Road toward Antrim.

They walked at a steady pace, although Herman's mind was skipping ahead to the chicken and gravy and chocolate cake he was sure were waiting for them at Rev. Brownlow's. The magical summer sky seemed very high above them as they walked and the watery greenness of the forest around them was shot with sparkling drops now and then, as a diving bird or an errant breeze shook free a cupped leaf or a loaded branch. Even Theo felt his heart lighter than it should have been, and Tommy walked steadily, his usually aching leg filled with strength.

When they reached Rev. Brownlow's, Mrs. Brownlow had finished making the gravy and was just about to call her family to dinner. Rev. Brownlow and his oldest son and daughter sat in the parlor, reading quietly. Three small boys and a girl hung idly on the porch railings or dangled their feet from the steps. Mrs. Brownlow saw the three brothers approaching shyly and waved to them warmly, including them in the call to eat as she passed her own children into the house.

The family gathered quietly around the table and Rev. Brownlow said a long, Sunday grace before they were served and began to eat.

"Is it all right, Father?" asked Mrs. Brownlow, wrinkling her brow.

"Excellent, Mother, excellent, as usual," said Rev. Brownlow heartily. Mrs. Brownlow knew his sermon had been a success and that not too many regular parishoners had been absent from church that morning. She settled back to enjoy the meal also.

After the last crumb of chocolate cake had disappeared, the children were sent to the porch where their older sister would read to them for an hour or so, until Mrs. Brownlow and their younger sister had finished the dishes. Then, everyone would take an afternoon nap. The younger boys found it hard to lie still, but they did their best and, though the nap hour passed very slowly, they were rewarded with apple pie and milk when they arose, and when evening services were over, they were allowed to return to their games of One Ole Cat and Run, Sheep, Run until night fell.

Rev. Brownlow ushered Theo and Tommy into the parlor and suggested that Herman might like to hear the stories sister was reading to the younger children. Herman hesitated, glowering in the door, but a fierce look from Theo sent him onto the porch.

"Boys," said Rev. Brownlow, "I have been asked to make you a business proposition and I hope you will give it careful thought before you give an answer." He paused and lighted a heavy, brown pipe. "That sounds pretty serious, doesn't it?" He smiled at the boys.

"I've been asked to make you a business proposition"

"Well, yes, sir," said Tommy uncomfortably.

"It needn't," said the minister. "I just wanted to hear how it would sound: heard Jim McDavitt say it one day and it sounded mighty impressive." He smiled at the boys again, and Theo smiled back uncertainly.

"It's this," Rev. Brownlow went on. "As you may know, Mr. Hanson, next farm to yours, isn't having an easy time."

"No, sir, he isn't," said Tommy. "We heard. . . ."

"Let Rev. Brownlow finish," said Theo interrupting.

"No, that's all right, Theodore. We've all heard, I guess. Seems like old Leander is right: burnt-over, logged-off land isn't much good. Anyway, Mr. Hanson's

199

wondering if he could rent some of your land and work it on shares. That is, pay the rent when the crops come in." He paused and set to work on his pipe again. Theo and Tommy sat quietly, not really looking at him now. Tangles of thoughts were in their minds and Rev. Brownlow knew this. He was giving them a few minutes to sort their ideas.

"Well, I expect you might wonder what will happen to you if you do this. I expect you're already thinking about how you can get Herman to school again this fall and how to work the farm and work on the beach, too." He stopped and puffed earnestly at the sluggish pipe. Theo nodded involuntarily and Tommy followed.

"Of course, you boys would still live in your cabin. Hanson's got a decent enough hut and is working on a better house now, so all he wants to rent, really, is the thirty acres on the north and the ten on the west, not counting the swamp." Tommy was surprised that Rev. Brownlow knew their land so well. Theo was sure Mr. Hanson had described it in detail and perhaps talked about it at some length with the minister.

"Herman could stay with us again; we'd be happy to have him and you could pay us twenty-five cents a week for his board and room, if you felt you had to." He puffed some more and Theo's forehead wrinkled.

"When would he want it, sir?"

"Well, he says you got a nice stand of corn there, but it needs tending and he says the same of your beans. He'd like to take over now and get out of it what he can — this'd save you having to work it the rest of the sum- mer — and he'd also like to thin out your cedar swamp and that little pine flat. He needs the fence posts and the firin' and he figures he can sell a couple of cords on the beach." Rev. Brownlow puffed some more, this time openly watching Theo and Tommy. "Oh, he'd pay something right away, in that case, and give you milk and eggs, too, if you need 'em."

"We do. Cow's dry," said Tommy, thinking aloud. He started at his own words when Theo poked him angrily.

Rev. Brownlow did not say anything to Tommy's statement, but said instead, "Well, you boys think it over, won't you? You can tell me your decision in a day or so. Mr. Hanson needs your help. There's no doubt of that and perhaps it might help you, too, I don't know."

"Yes, sir, we'll come in and tell you on Tuesday," said Theo in a precise manner. He stood up and pulled Tommy to his feet also.

"No hurry, boys," said the man, getting slowly to his feet. "You'll stay a while, surely? Oh, and I want to tell you how much everyone admires you lads."

"What?" said Theo.

"Oh, yes. You know, taking hold so well after your father died and seeing to the farm and looking after Herman. Even sending him to school!" Rev. Brownlow sucked fiercely on the pipe again and then stuffed it roughly in his jacket pocket.

"Why, sir? I mean, why should anybody think it's so much?" Tommy spoke breathlessly.

"Why? Why, because I don't know any other boys around here that could have done the same! And neither does anyone else. Why, I was talking to Supervisor Mc-Davitt just yesterday, and he said. . . ."

But the boys were not listening to what Mr. McDavitt had said. Rev. Brownlow had said enough and they looked at each other with shining eyes.

18
Theo Closes a Deal

"No!!!" shouted Herman. His voice rang through the trees as his brothers walked home from Rev. Brownlow's.

Tommy looked cxasperated and Theo irritated, but they held their peace and let Herman pour out his feelings. Both felt fatherly and patient at the moment.

"I won't! It's awful living there! It's too hot at night and I gotta wash all the time and besides, it isn't fair!" Tears were in his eyes now and he let them stream down his face without concealment.

"But you like the Brownlows, don't you?" asked Tommy gently.

"No! I hate them!"

"Stop!" said Theo firmly. "Now you're talking like a baby and you know it! They're kind and they like you and you know it! You must go to school. You must." The last words were an urgent plea.

Herman's sobs calmed greatly now.

"Why?" he asked grumpily.

"How far do you think Tommy and I can go in this world with almost no learning at all?"

"Yes, but you could be a big man, maybe postmaster or a foreman," Tommy said, and skipped a step, laughing. "And then you could keep us in our old age."

Theo laughed too, and Herman smiled a short, watery smile.

"Well," said Theo, "let's wait, anyhow, until after supper to talk about it."

The boys had reached their own yard now and all three stopped for a minute and looked at their farm.

The tall trees that had been left near the house seemed soft and warm in the afternoon summer sun. The cabin itself looked solid, as if it had grown, almost, from the ground. The barn stood on slightly higher ground and to the south a bit. In back of the barn the glossy green of the pasture rose to the top of a hill where a little grove marked the summit. The sun at their backs, the boys could see clearly the two small, white crosses that stood outside the pasture fence on the south, just at the edge of the little grove. They stood silently for a moment and then, just as quietly, walked across the yard and into their cabin.

That evening the boys rested, Herman stretched on his stomach before a small fire. The evening was cool and it would be good to climb into bed feeling warm and drowsy. Also, although the door had been open to the sunny world all day, the house still seemed damp from the rain the day before.

Tommy was beginning to have doubts about Rev. Brownlow's plan and gazed frowning into the fire.

"Well, what do you think?" asked Theo when the brothers had been quiet for some time.

"Oh, I suppose we've got to," said Herman. His chin resting on his fists made his head bounce up and down as he spoke.

"What? Why have you changed your mind?" asked Tommy.

"Oh, well, school's not bad. And the food is good. And my feet stay warm. Mostly."

"Do you think we should, Tommy?" asked Theo.

"Oh, yes, I guess," answered Tommy reluctantly, "but I don't like giving up Papa's farm!"

"It isn't giving it up, stupid! You know it's only for a little while. A year, or two, at the most."

"Still. . . ."

"And Rev. Brownlow said Mr. Hanson needed it. He did."

"Is it true, d'ya think?" asked Herman.

"I guess he wouldn't say anything untrue," said Theo in a scandalized tone.

"Well, we can go see him, anyway, and maybe find out," said Tommy.

"Just think," said Theo softly, "in two years I'll be a man, and we'll have enough saved so I can hire some help. . . ."

". . . and we can get some chickens again. . . . ," added Tommy.

". . . and maybe get the thresher to come here!" finished Herman triumphantly.

"Let's go to bed now and we can go see Rev. Brownlow tomorrow, after supper," said Tommy.

"Let's think about it overnight," said Theo. "If Mr. Hanson is just doing us a favor, we don't want it. We can get along fine without help."

205

Herman looked at him in amazement.

"So," continued Theo, "before we see Rev. Brownlow, we should go see Mr. Hanson. We'll stay home tomorrow, even if they blow for us."

"Not answer the work whistle? But we might lose about fifty cents that way!" exclaimed Tommy.

"Can't be helped. This is more important." Theo rose and scattered the ashes of the fire. They would build a new one in the morning, or, more likely, eat a cold breakfast. Maybe, maybe, they could buy an old stove some day. His eyes wandered up the huge stone chimney, looking for a likely place for a stove pipe.

"Well, then," said Tommy from the foot of the ladder, "come along and stop dreaming."

The next morning, after they had finished their chores, the boys started down the Flat Road toward the Hansons. When they were halfway there, they heard the shrill call of the schooner whistle, calling men to the beaches for loading. Every day at this time of year there was one boat, often more, waiting for lumber. Wrinkles of worry creased Theo's forehead at the thought of the work he and Tommy would not be doing today and he hoped that his decision was the right one.

The entrance to the Hanson farm had been cut through the scrub growth that covered most of the farm-

land near the road. The tracks ran back to a very small clearing about two hundred feet from the road. The Hansons' cabin was tiny and Herman thought it could hardly be called a house. It had a shed roof and the logs were liberally chinked with sod and moss. Mr. Hanson had not wasted much time putting up the cabin, but Theo sympathized; after all, they had arrived in the spring and the work of the farm was waiting to be done all the time Mr. Hanson was building the cabin. The scrub pines and wild cherries were scarcely taller than the house and the tarred roof shone wetly in the summer sun.

As the boys came nearer the little house, Mrs. Hanson stepped from the doorway. She had quite obviously come to greet them and Theo wondered how she knew they had come. She wiped her hands down the sides of her apron and waved and smiled.

"Hello, boys! Heard you comin'! C'mon in and have a cuppa coffee. The mister'll be in in a minute. I sent the girl to get him."

Theo, Tommy, and Herman followed Mrs. Hanson into the dark, low room that was the cabin. The room was crowded with beds, chairs and a large, ornate round dining table. Theo knew the Hansons had had a larger house where they had come from.

The boys sat around the table, Herman swinging his legs awkwardly. In a little while, Mr. Hanson appeared and Mrs. Hanson put mugs of steaming coffee in front of each one.

"I 'spect you've come about the proposition I made to you through the reverend." Mr. Hanson looked at them steadily over the edge of his mug.

"Yessir, yes, we have," said Theo and cleared his throat.

"Don't, now," said Mr. Hanson, surprisingly, and raised his hand, "don't say another word until I've told you my offer."

Tommy nodded, then Herman and Theo.

"This is it: 'til the crops come in and I clear some lumber, half a pail of milk a day, two dozen eggs and a pound of butter a week, and firewood too, if you'll help with the cuttin' of it on Saturday's." He peered anxiously into the boys' faces. "Then, in the fall, I give you half what I get for the crops — seein' as you did put 'em in — and one quarter what we get for the lumber, minus what you've took out for firin'." He laid his hand resoundingly on the table, and sat still, his lips compressed. Mrs. Hanson shook her head wonderingly behind him.

Herman looked trustingly at Theo, but Tommy looked wildly around, his face red. Then Theo spoke, quietly and confidently and Tommy turned to him in amazement.

"It sounds fine, Mr. Hanson. How long do you want this to go on?"

"Well, that's a good sharp question, lad. The arrangements I mentioned are just for this year, but I'm sure I'll need to rent your land again next year. But since things'll be different then, why don't we wait 'til then to figure 'em out. It'll be fair, it'll be fair," he ended emphatically.

"I'm sure, Mr. Hanson. That's fine then, isn't it, boys?" Theo turned to Tommy and Herman, who stared at him a second, their jaws dropping.

"Yes, it's fine, Mr. Hanson." Theo drank his coffee down and rose. "Do we need a paper of any kind?" A worried note crept into his voice.

"Not for me, son. Your hand's good enough for me. I hope it's the same with you?" He stood waiting for Theo's answer.

"Of course, of course," said Theo eagerly and held out his hand. Mr. Hanson shook it vigorously and then turned and shook hands with Tommy and Herman.

"Well, now that you men've settled all the business, how about a piece of apple pie?" Mrs. Hanson broke in with a wide smile.

"Yes, ma'am," said Herman, sitting down promptly and pulling his chair back up to the table. Tommy and Mr. Hanson laughed and Theo smiled, and all of them sat down with Herman.

When the pie was gone and Theo and Tommy knew it was time to leave, Mrs. Hanson followed them down the path a little ways and then handed Herman a roughly made basket with a clean, faded pink dishcloth covering the contents. It smelled like a bakery shop and Herman smiled warmly at Mrs. Hanson.

"Thank you, Mrs. Hanson, thank you so much!" he said.

"Yes, ma'am!" said Theo and Tommy together.

"That's all right, boys. Take care of yourselves. G'bye!"

"'Bye," said all three and waved as she hurried back into the cabin.

When the boys reached their own cabin, Theo took charge of the basket and put it carefully on the top shelf of the corner cupboard.

"For supper," he said with authority, and Tommy only groaned.

209

Later that day Rev. Brownlow came to visit, while Theo was on the roof with his pile of shingles, fixing the leak.

"Hi, up there!" the minister called.

Theo waved, his mouth full of shingle nails.

"Hear you decided to rent the farm!"

Theo nodded and Tommy, sitting idly on the ridge pole, answered, "Yes, we did, sir!"

Theo took the nails from his mouth and put them in his pocket. Then he climbed down.

"We are very grateful to you, sir, for . . . well, for telling us . . . for help. . . ."

"He means," said Tommy sliding down the roof and landing with a thump beside his brother, "that we thank you for telling us about Mr. Hanson and how he wanted our farm. To rent, that is."

"Glad I could help you, boys. How does Herman feel about it?" he said, watching the youngest brother's slight figure moving beside the barn where he was gathering an armload of firewood.

"Well. . . ," Theo began.

Rev. Brownlow laughed.

"I think I understand," he said. "Well, you've done what's best all along, Theodore. I'm certain you will now, too."

"Oh, yes, sir. He'll go to school this fall. And, if it's still all right, board with you this winter."

"Of course, I said it was and I meant it."

". . . but," went on Theo, firmly, "summer after next we should have saved enough to farm the place as it should be, so I hope Mr. Hanson will understand we can't rent it to him then."

"I'm sure he understands. Oh, he's a man with a lot

of ideas and intends planting cherry trees, you know. Guess he already has, in fact. Won't bear for some years, o' course, but in the meantime he's gonna farm some of his own land as soon's he can get it ready. This way, using your farm, he can do that in his own time and still get his trees started, too."

"He'll be busy," said Tommy seriously.

"That he will, but *you* know how it is when you're trying to keep a farm going," said Rev. Brownlow.

Theo's back straightened and Tommy stood beside him solemnly.

"We certainly do, sir."

"Oh, I almost forgot. I brought you something," said the minister, and handed Theo a small magazine. Theo looked puzzled.

"Thought Herman might read to you and you should practice, Tommy." Theo looked puzzled, but took the magazine.

"Thank you, sir," he said.

"Well, got to be going, boys. G'bye and God bless you, all of you, you're a credit to your father's memory and fine young men."

"Good-bye, sir," said Tommy and Theo in unison.

They stood a little taller as the big figure in black strode down the yard and out to the Flat Road, which was dancing with shadows under the high gold of the sun.

Fixing the leak

19
A Shiny Tomorrow

That evening the three boys sat on a bench outside the door of their cabin. Herman and Tommy were watching and hearing and smelling the summer evening. Theo was pouring over the magazine Rev. Brownlow had brought. There were stories with pictures that maddened Theo because he could not read the stories. In the back, there were many advertisements and he had turned to these.

"*We sell only reliable and well-tested instruments!*"
"*. . . quality is more important than price. . . .*"
"*Plows, built for strength. Price: $2.33.*"
"What're you looking at, Theo?" asked Herman.
"Ummmm?" asked Theo.
"I said, what're you looking at?"
"Oh, just this." He showed the advertisement to Herman.

"That's a good one, isn't it?" said Tommy, looking over his brother's shoulder.

"Yes, and year after next we'll need one like it."

"But look how much it costs!" cried Herman.

"I know, I know," said Theo soothingly. "I can read numbers, you know."

"But . . . but how can we ever buy it?" Herman's face was pinched with worry. Tommy said nothing, but also looked at his older brother for an answer.

Theo closed the magazine and put it on the bench beside him. He lifted his chin and sniffed the air. The air was full of summer smells: wet leaf mold on the forest floor, ripe hay from the open loft door, wet seaweed from the mess of fish Leander had left that afternoon, a faint, peaceful smoke from the Hansons' kitchen fire, blown up from the south.

Theo shook his head vigorously and laughed and turned to his brothers.

"Yes, we can buy it. Not now, of course. But Tom and I will work and we can save money. We won't be boys forever. Soon I'll be a man, and then you two will in your turn."

"You're always saying you are a man now," Herman sniffed.

Theo laughed.

"I know, but I guess I know better, now."

"You mean we can buy it on our own?" asked Tommy, going back to the plow.

"Yes, but that doesn't mean . . . well, it doesn't mean we couldn't let Mrs. Hanson give us doughnuts. . . ."

"I'll say," said Herman softly, remembering what had been in the basket.

"It just means, we do the best we can with the things that come along."

214

"In a few years, maybe, we can have a team of horses," said Tommy exuberantly.

"Maybe so," said Theo, "but now we have to think just about working on the beach. And you, maybe, if you're good enough in school," he said, turning to Herman, "you could get a job in the lumber office. So, you just think about school."

". . . and what about some pigs?" said Tommy, "maybe a half a dozen, or so?"

"Maybe an iron stove for the kitchen," said Herman.

" . . . and a hired hand," said Tommy.

"Stop!" said Theo loudly. "Right now, we won't think of any of those things. Now we just think of working on the beach and going to school. That's all! Do you hear? All!" Herman and Tommy were startled because Theo spoke with great vehemence. They fell silent and

"Maybe an iron stove"

watched the sun redden in the west and then sink behind the guardian pines, leaving a billowing lavender path across the bay, glittering through the trunks of the massive trees.

"Time for bed," said Theo shortly. Herman was crest-fallen and felt as if the glory of their victory had been snatched from him.

He felt Tommy nudge him and looked back. Tommy was pointing at Theo.

Theo, a step ahead of them, climbing to the loft, held the magazine with its shining picture of a plow tightly to his chest. There were stars in his eyes and he smiled softly to himself.

Herman and Tommy felt the reflection of that smile on their own faces.

THE END

GLOSSARY

cant hook — A pole with a curved, movable hook, used for handling logs.

lighter — A kind of barge, often equipped with cranes, etc., used to carry goods to and from larger ships lying at distance from a wharf.

Manitou (Man-e-too) — Gitche Manitou was the Great Spirit of the Chippewas, while Mitchi Manitou was the evil spirit. Kewadin, a real Indian who lived until 1884, was thought to be the representative of Mitchi Manitou and was held in great awe by the Indians living around Torch Lake.

mattock — Shaped like a pickaxe, this tool has blades instead of points. It is used for grubbing and cutting in the ground.

peavy — An iron-pointed lever with a movable hook extending around the point.

wangan or wanigan (won-gun or won-e-gun) — A raft, or flat-bottomed boat, used to carry a kitchen to cook for the loggers working on a river drive. It was usually pulled by another vessel.

COLOPHON

Published by William B. Eerdmans Publishing Company, Grand Rapids, Michigan.

Illustrations, book design, and jacket by Betty Beeby. Composed in 12 pt. linotype Baskerville on 14 pt. body, with numerals set in 18 pt. Chisel Wide and titles set in 18 pt. Baskerville Roman ATF.

Offset by Grand Rapids Book Manufacturers, Inc. on 60 lb. Warren Old Style made by S. D. Warren Paper Company, Boston, Massachusetts.

End papers: Slate Blue Talisman Text by Simpson Lee Paper Company, Vicksburg, Michigan.

Bound by William B. Eerdmans Printing Company, Grand Rapids, Michigan, in Arrestox C 53320 made by Joseph Bancroft & Sons Company, New York and Chicago.